She could have stopped him. She could have yanked out of his hold and run. She could have stopped him before when they were still in the open, surrounded by other people. She could have . . . but she didn't. He was taking her into his arms; he was bending to brush his lips against hers. She knew it and allowed it, nay, she asked for it, as her hands wrapped around his neck and her supple body pressed against him. . . .

LADY BELL

Claudette Williams

FAWCETT CREST • NEW YORK

A Fawcett Crest Book
Published by Ballantine Books
Copyright © 1986 by Claudette Williams

Library of Congress Catalog Card Number: 86-90879

ISBN: 0-449-20752-8

Manufactured in the United States of America

First Edition: July 1986

To my uncle Eddie with love—
Because when I fondly think of my youth, I think of him.

Chapter One

Cullingham Grange reposed sedately in the Cotswolds. Its tenant farmers enjoyed a good living, as did their baron, the young Sir Robert of Cullingham. He had inherited the grange, the title, and a modest income at the age of thirteen, when both his parents were killed at sea. Along with these responsibilities was yet another, the guardianship of his sister, Arabella, then only ten years old.

Eleven years had passed since their parents' deaths, and Cullingham Grange was just as successful and fruitful as it had always been. Due to their circumstances, brother and sister had developed a very close bond only recently threatened. The threat? Why, a man. A man whose image glittered in Arabella's dark eyes.

Into Bell Cullingham's life entered a gentleman of no mean order. He was handsome, he was masculine in all ways, he was charming, and, added to these attributes was the fact that he sported the uniform of the Hussar so very well. Robby took one look at him and warned his sister in the strictest tone that this Colonel Holding was nothing but a rake. Robby's closest friend, Freddy Eastdean, attempted to reason with Bell. He cajoled, hinted, and then blatantly wagged the finger of doom at her, but Bell heard only the sound of her own young and innocent heart. It leaped, it pounded, it sang—all because of the charming colonel. He teased her, he flirted with her, and he made her feel the woman she had grown to be. And he was everything Robby and Freddy predicted he would be.

There was no gainsaying that Arabella was the fairest girl in the Cotswolds. Why, her amber curls glinted in the sunlight and wooed a man to stare. Her dark eyes, almond-shaped and darkly lashed had warmed many a man's dreams. Her nose was pert, her lips full and cherry-ripe, and her figure, though petite, was provocative enough to taunt even a saintly fellow into naughty fantasy. In addition, she was lively, outspoken, unspoiled, and innocent.

Colonel Holding noticed her at once. He had no sooner entered the Cotswolds with his regiment than he spotted Arabella, and so began their dance. His reputation was well known to Sir Robert, who watched him with a knowing eye. The colonel, he correctly surmised, was taken with the pretty Bell, but not overset. The time came for the dance to end and the colonel to leave. So Sir Robert and his friend Freddy stood back and waited to catch Bell as she fell, and fall she did!

Sir Robert and Freddy waited in the Cullingham library, a lovely room with all its windows overlooking the finely landscaped grange park. The library door opened, and Freddy's hazel eyes met Robby's dark ones before they turned to find Arabella—quite dashing in her black velvet riding habit—standing somberly in the doorway.

"Well, don't stand there like a stock," said her brother. "Come in. We've been waiting for you half the morning!"

The serious expression vanished as a sparkle of mischief entered Arabella's dark eyes. "And what, pray, were you doing the other half?"

Freddy eyed her doubtfully and turned to Robby, "Know what? Don't think she is going into a decline. What say you, ol' boy?"

Miss Cullingham cast both young men a withering look.

"A decline? Me? Over that . . . that . . . *nothing* of a man?"

Her brother pulled a face. "Oh, *now* he is nothing, eh? Wasn't more than a day ago when he was the sun, the moon, and the stars?"

"Was he, by Jove?" put in Freddy, struck by this notion.

"No!" answered Miss Cullingham from a higher plane. "No, he wasn't, isn't . . . and . . . and I . . ." She moved across the room now and pulled off her kid gloves to stand facing the fire, her back to them. In truth, she was hurting. Her youthful pride had received a smashing blow. Her inclination to optimism had been sadly shaken and her trust in men misplaced. She couldn't finish the sentence.

Her brother frowned and moved to her. "Bell . . . ? It doesn't matter. Trouble is . . . the whole thing is my fault."

She turned to eye him in some surprise. "Your fault? How can you say so when you warned me of him from the start?"

"My fault we weren't in London. My fault . . . you didn't have a London season. I should have taken you there . . . should have arranged to present you. I suppose I was selfish. Wanted . . . to keep you here at Cullingham . . . with me. Hoped you would marry one of m'friends and we would be comfortable. . . ."

Freddy suddenly took on a look of terror. What was this? Robby wanted her to marry one of his friends? Well, as he considered himself on top of this list, his nerves began to jingle. It wasn't that he didn't adore Arabella—for indeed, he did—but not in a romantic fashion. Besides, he was not in the petticoat line, and the thought of marriage to *anyone* absolutely horrified him. As he choked on words he could not express, both Cullinghams burst into indecent mirth.

"Rest easy, ol' boy," said Robby, patting him on the shoulder. "Didn't have you in mind."

3

Relief flooded Freddy's cheeks, but then he was assailed with yet another concern. "What do you mean, not me? Who, then?"

"Well, I always thought that William and Bell . . ." started Robby.

"William?" ejaculated Arabella indignantly. "What ever made you think I would have such a clod?"

"I say," added Freddy. "That is coming on a bit strong. *William*, over me?"

"Well . . . but Bell always seemed to *like* him . . ." returned Robby, surprised at their heat.

"There is a great deal of difference between liking and loving. And besides, I don't precisely like him," said Arabella, thinking to herself that at one time she had thought William of Heathrow quite attractive. However, at the time she had been twelve and he sixteen.

"It doesn't make a ha'porth of difference!" said Robby, growing weary of the discussion. "Mean to do the right thing by you, m'girl. As a matter of fact, have been working on it for weeks. . . ."

"Ay." Freddy nodded. "Ever since you stood up for two dances with Holding at the assembly."

Arabella's hands went to her hips, but her brother put up his hand to forestall her. "Take a damper, Bell. I wasn't wrong about him, now was I?"

Sadly, he had not been wrong. The dashing colonel had stolen a few kisses, had filled her eyes with stars, and had promptly moved on to his next conquest, telling her that he was not the marrying kind. She sighed and, incurably honest with herself, replied, "Right, then."

"As I was saying. We sent Jenkins to lease a town house for the season and, by Jove, if he hasn't established us in Grovesnor Square. Sent for Aunt Violet, who will meet us there and act as chaperone for you. . . ."

"Chaperone? But Robby . . . I have you," she surprised herself by stating.

4

He laughed. "So you have, but you need a female that travels in the *ton* set . . . get you a voucher to Almacks . . . take you to Bond Street shops. Anyway, you like the ol' girl . . ."

"Yes, I do, but . . . I am one and twenty, after all, and I hardly think . . ."

"Freddy comes with us, and I daresay we shall do, right and tight, eh, Freddy?" proceeded Sir Robert, waving away her objection.

"Ay," Freddy nodded.

Arabella's dark eyes lit with anticipation, and she moved to throw her arms around her brother, "Oh Robby . . . thank you."

"That's a girl." He snapped his fingers in the air. "So much for Colonel Holding. We Cullinghams are made of strong and sturdy stuff."

"So we are," she laughed. "When do we leave?"

He looked at his friend, "What say you to the morning?"

Freddy shook his head. "Can't be thinking."

"What do you mean?" returned Robby, taking umbrage.

"Cock fight tomorrow afternoon. Percy's gray against the Great Red."

Robby remembered. "Right. Leave immediately after. Stop at that little inn, The Red Bull, on the Thames. Bell will like that. Start out early the next morning."

Thus, it was agreed.

Chapter Two

Overlooking the Thames, just outside Dorchester, reposed a richly landscaped estate. It belonged to one Sir Jasper Standon. The library of Standon Grange was nicely appointed with its huge lead-paned, bowed window overlooking the serpentine portion of the Thames that meandered through the estate. Shaun Standon, the tenth earl of Magdalen, stood with his hands clasped tightly at his back and contemplated the green landscape, wondering what in thunder he was doing there!

Sir Jasper sat in a slumped position, watching his great-nephew through sharp gray eyes as he pulled at his lower lip. He was seventy and quite used to having his own way, which is what he wanted now. How to bring it about with his nephew was more than he could fathom at the moment. The very thing he admired in Shaun Standon was the fact that the lad was his own man. The tenth earl of Magdalen was nine and twenty, a handsome devil with a will and mind that rarely could be wielded by another's whims.

Sir Jasper sighed and attempted feebly, "Don't see that I've asked anything untowards. . . ." He waited for Shaun to turn and look at him. That the earl's deep blue eyes were *not* twinkling spurred him on, and he put an aged white hand to his forehead. "Certes, lad . . . I *am* dying, you know."

6

Now the deep blue eyes twinkled. "There is not the slightest doubt in my mind that you will outlive us all." He put up his hand to stall his great-uncle. "Uncle . . . what you ask is impossible."

"Damnation! This sort of thing is done all the time." Sir Jasper was frowning darkly. "It isn't as though you have formed an attachment elsewhere. . . ?" The question was there.

An attachment? The tenth earl of Magdalen contemplated the old man in front of him for a long moment before answering. There was a time when his entire world had centered on one frail being. She had given her heart and hand to some country boy and vanished from his life. No. He had not formed an attachment elsewhere. It was an emotion he carefully guarded himself against.

"That has nothing to do with it," the earl answered gravely. He put a hand through his raven locks, and his blue eyes were alert. He wanted an end to this discussion. He would never have come had he realized this was what his uncle had in mind. "Now, my tyrant, I must go. I am promised at the Bull."

"Damn it, boy!" the older man snapped, speaking to the earl as though he were ten and not nine and twenty. "Why should you stay at the village inn when you can stay here?"

"Because my friends are there, and *they* won't try and foist marriage onto me. Besides, we are entered at Percy Harley's for the cock fight."

"Oh?" said the old squire, his interest caught and neatly diverted. "Harley putting up his gray?"

"Ay, against Brickley's red."

"Well, well." However, the squire could be tenacious at times, and he waved this off. "Never mind all that now. I am going to put it to you this way, Shaun. Marry my ward, and see to it she is comfortably installed in London, where she can enjoy life. She is a good child, and, though

7

she ain't exactly biddable, she is sensible and won't be getting in the way of your . . . pleasures. She has a good head on her shoulders and a steady temper. Do this, and I will leave her everything I possess. . . . And don't be telling me *you* don't need it. I know that very well. But the thing is, *she* does, and she won't get it unless you marry her!'' He put up his hand to stall his nephew's reply. ''I mean it, Shaun. She would be a pauper without the provisions I can install for her in my will.'' He eyed his nephew from shrewd discerning eyes and knew he had angered him.

Shaun Standon drew himself up to his full height, which was considerable. He squared his shoulders, and his blue Irish eyes were militant in their angry glitter. His mouth was set, and the words were nearly a hiss. ''Remember this, Uncle. Yours is the action; let yours be the fault!'' It was all he was going to say. As far as he was concerned, the matter was closed. He turned on his heel, scooped up his driving coat, hat, and gloves from a nearby wall table, and stampeded out the door, calling to the butler for his phaeton to be brought around.

Sir Jasper sat in some frustration and watched his great-nephew's exit. He knew he had pushed him too far too soon. Shaun had a good heart beneath his cold exterior. He wouldn't want to see Rose go into a poorhouse—but neither would he be led where he had no desire to go. That was the problem.

What to do? He had said he would leave her penniless, but that was not something he could do. It had been an idle threat. Had Shaun known this? Perhaps. What to do now? Drat it all; he needed a solution. He wanted his Rose safely wed before he went to his maker, and he wanted her wed to Shaun.

The library door opened softly, and a tall, shapely girl of twenty-one years entered. Her heart-shaped face was framed with short, tawny curls. Her eyes were hazel, with soft brown brows and lashes. Her nose was upturned, her lips prettily formed. She eyed her guardian with total understanding and said with a gentle tone not untouched with amusement, "Ah. He did not fall in with your schemes." It was a statement.

"Be still! I am thinking," he returned tartly, and pulled at his lower lip.

"There is nothing to think about," she returned, not in the least disturbed by his harsh sounding words. She knew her guardian all too well.

She was wrong, though, for what he allowed from her, he would not allow from others. She was the daughter of his closest friend and of the woman, the only woman, he had fancied himself in love with all those years ago. When her parents died in poverty, Sir Jasper had scooped up Rose and made her his own. "My own brat," he said, almost absently. "Need you settled. Don't you see that? No, you don't." He shook his head. "Should have seen to your ball. . . ."

"But, dearest, you gave me a lovely ball only last year . . ." she started in some surprise.

"Ay. With the locals—I mean, I should have presented you in London. You would have taken . . . and made a good match. As it is . . ." His voice drifted off. He was seventy, and while he knew he was not about to die on the morrow, he also knew that he would eventually. He wanted her settled before that happened. He wanted to see her happy and safe. He didn't want her living a spinster's life in the country . . . alone, as he had been. He would have to convince her that he would leave her penniless if she did not agree to his dictums.

"Fond of you, girl. You know that." He didn't wait for her reply. "But I swear, if you don't marry that devil nevvy of mine, I'll cut you off without a sou!" He pulled a face and looked away.

She laughed. "Well, that is fine speaking. Number one,

dearest, I don't want your money. I have been fortunate all these years, for I could have led a most uncomfortable youth had you not seen fit to care for me. If I must make my way in the world, I shall contrive to do so, for even if I were willing to marry Shaun, which I am not, you, even you, cannot force him to propose to me.''

''Contrive, eh?'' He eyed her. ''I have no doubt you might try, but it wouldn't be easy. You'll marry him.'' His mind went to another time, to friends of another era, and suddenly a notion took hold and he sparkled. ''Have it! Go on. . . . Leave me be. . . .''

She eyed him warily. ''Have what?''

''Never you mind!''

''Darling Jasper . . . what are you going to do?''

''I may have closeted m'self here in the country, but have a friend or two that still wield some power over the *haute ton* in London. Violet Cullingham. I'll send you to my own dear Vi!''

Chapter Three

A traveler on his way out of the Cotswolds heading in an easterly direction toward London might encounter the charming village of Dorchester. A quiet town, Dorchester was dominated by its magnificent Roman church, which stood at the far end of the town square. The church sported a three-story porch, which could be easily viewed in the distance by any passerby. The town itself was quaintly designed and ornamented by a brilliant display of white birch lining its main avenue.

The Bull Tavern rested sedately at the village tip and overlooked the winding Thames River. The inn did a modest business and catered to the aristocracy as a rule. However, on this day the Bull Tavern fairly rang with the clatter of excitement and riotous sporting gentlemen. Aristocrats, merchants, wealthy cits young and old, had gathered at the Dorchester's only inn in order to catch the famed cock fight due to take place that very afternoon. As it happened, there were not enough rooms to be had and most of these gentlemen found themselves scampering around the countryside in an attempt to bespeak accommodations for the evening. The Bull's main room was filled to overflowing with zealous sportsmen ready to toast one another with bumpers of ale. The mood was gay and definitely masculine.

Sir Robert Cullingham and his good friend Mr. Eastdean

11

arrived with their charge, Arabella, in time to see that this was a lively establishment that promised to be most amusing. However, both young men saw at once that it was *not* the place for a lady of quality to be freely roaming about. What to do? They had bespoken rooms long in advance at the inn. Their horses were in need of a night's rest, and there wasn't another inn for some distance. They looked at each other and Sir Robert turned to advise her in warning tones, "Bell . . . must see you have to stay in your room."

"Must see?" she repeated before her hands went to her hips and her dark eyes lit with the challenge. "No, my darling Robby, I don't see at all."

"Bell . . . just look. . . . You don't want to be ogled by such a set. Everyone seems to be . . . well . . . just a bit jolly."

"In their cups," she said with a laugh. "Yes, I do see, and of course I won't go into the tavern, but you can't mean to keep me confined in my room either. Why, the town is lovely, and I mean to do a little exploring."

They ushered her between them up the stairs to a pretty little room decorated in quiet shades of blue. "Look, Bell . . . such a nice room . . . take a book; read. You like to read," said her brother.

"So I do, and so I shall . . ." responded Arabella Cullingham, pulling herself up to her full five feet two inches and glaring, " . . . when I choose to do so." Then, staying him with an uplifted hand, she proceeded. "Look, Robby, I have been in a closed carriage for hours and hours while you and Freddy rode your horses."

"We put them at the back . . . didn't we? We kept you company," objected her brother, incensed.

"Yes, for all of thirty minutes!" she snapped, not at all appeased. "Now you two shall go off again and that is as it should be. Far be it from me to demand you keep me company, but at least—at least allow me to take a walk

12

about town. The evening promises to be dull enough for me."

This did the trick. Robby and Freddy eyed each other guiltily and Freddy said grandly, "Has a point there."

"Ay, fastest little talker . . . always has been," Robby conceded ruefully. "Right, then . . . a little walk about town." He frowned. All their servants had gone on ahead to London a day before, and he had not thought to retain Bella's maid. He didn't like her going about alone, but the village seemed sober enough. After all, all the sporting chaps were gathered below. She was such a wild thing. He had always taken pride in her rough-and-tumble ways, allowing her freedom, allowing her to roam the Cotswolds on her horse without the benefit of a groom in attendance. He could hardly expect her to change now, overnight, could he? He sighed, touched her delicate shoulder, and cautioned, "Then you won't be gone long?"

She was an affectionate soul and was softened immediately by his gentle concern. "No, just long enough to stretch my legs and get the kinks of traveling out of me. There . . . you two, go off and enjoy yourselves. I mean to wash up and change this crumpled up gown of mine."

Some forty minutes later Miss Arabella Cullingham was fetchingly attired in a blue silk gown with a waisted and matching spencer jacket. A blue silk chip hat with netting and fine silk bows adorned her flounce of amber curls. Kid gloves and half boots made up the remainder of her attire, and she drew more than a few glances as she made her way out the back door of the inn.

The church was taken by storm. She purchased a guide book that drew a history of the church and town both, and she perused this with interest as she meandered through its wide halls. Some thirty minutes passed before she discovered the church's rear courtyard. She walked through and stopped to pet a grizzled old gray cat when she observed a swan waddle down an enbankment and take to the water. With a crow of delight she followed and watched as birds, ducks, and various wild fowl played in the Thames River.

She sighed to see the day fast turning into dusk and it was time to return to the inn. She picked her way through a small thicket of woods and found as she reached the roadway that a thorny vine had wrapped itself about her shoulders. Carefully she attempted to disentangle herself without tearing her silk, and as she had the last of it done, she flung it away and stepped onto the road..

Shaun Standon, tenth earl of Magdalen, tooled his perfectly matched pair of dapple grays on the dusty road toward Dorchester with no uncertain skill and precision. He was a notable whip and a bruising rider to hounds. He had left his little tiger to relax in the Bull's stableyard when he had gone off to his uncle's earlier, and, therefore, had no one now at his back. Like his horses, his phaeton was built for speed, and his mood was paced for the same. He was in the devil of a temper, for his great-uncle had attempted to force his hand, and this was something he would not allow. At the same time, he had always rather liked young Rose and did not want to see her hurt in this affair. His great-uncle might just carry out his threat and leave her without a sou to her name. In this state of mind he drove his team hard and fast. So when an object in blue appeared before their fiery eyes, the pair of grays spooked sharply to the left, demanding all of the driver's skill to keep his vehicle from landing in the roadside ditch!

Arabella screeched, was thrown off balance, and fell back into the thorny vine once again. Meanwhile, the gentleman in the phaeton called down curses upon everything in sight.

"Just like all your kind!" Shaun Standon said harshly as he jumped down from his vehicle to quiet his team. "Never was there a female with an ounce of common sense!'' he ranted as he petted and soothed his pair of spirited geldings into a calmer state.

At first Arabella had been too surprised by the incident, and too busy extricating herself once again from the sticky vines to notice the driver. However, at this last she turned, her hands on her hips and her dark eyes flashing to meet the challenge. The fact that here was an exceptionally handsome man of some stature and fashion registered vaguely. But she could not help noticing as he flung his top hat to the seat, that his raven waves of hair glistened in the sunlight and that his deep blue eyes were filled with anger. This, however, did not stop her from advising him, ''Common sense, my good sir, dictates that one does not drive at a reckless speed 'round a bend so very near a village, where anything or anyone might spook such fine animals!''

Her spirited rebuke brought his deep blue eyes to inspect her further. Bell was now removing the last of the vine, which had sent her hat askew and ripped at her silk spencer. She was unable to control her anger.

''Drat! Double drat! Now see what you have made me do!''

Seeing her distress, he softened, and now that his team was standing quietly, he went forward to help her.

''You are, of course, quite right. The fault was mine,'' he said graciously, for it occurred to him that here was the finest piece of little muslin he had ever clapped eyes on. Her piquant face was most attractive; her figure alluring enough to already stir his imagination. As she had no maid in attendance, he took her for some country merchant's daughter, and, therefore, fair game!

His pretty apology soothed her into conceding, ''No, no, I should not have stepped into the road like that. If your horses had sustained an injury, I . . .'' All at once she found herself being taken into a strong embrace and stopped mid-sentence to look in some surprise at his face.

His voice was tinged with amusement. ''Then both having pledged our apologies to each other, there is but one thing left to do." So saying, he did it. His kiss was meant to be a flirtatious gesture, a form of entertainment, a way to forget the trials of an uncomfortable afternoon. Yet somehow he found himself stirred by the pressure of her provocative body twisting against his own, and without his meaning to, his mouth parted her lips and his tongue teased hers.

She was startled by his embrace and did not at first think to object. She was amazed by his kiss and thought perhaps he was mad and the best thing to do would be to stand stock still, when she suddenly became aware of the thrill that rushed through her body. She made an attempt to pull out of his hold, but he held her in a steel grip. Her hand moved to push at his hard chest, and suddenly he released her. She stood, her cheeks on fire, her dark eyes blazing, and her voice lost somewhere in her throat.

As she sought to bring words to her lips, he was once again on the attack, scooping her up this time into his arms like a babe, and saying lightly, "Lord, woman, don't struggle, or I shall drop you." With that he lifted her with ease onto the upholstered chair of his phaeton.

"What the deuce do you think you are doing?" demanded Arabella, at last finding her voice. "Are you mad?"

He grinned at her as he took up the reins and said easily, "You don't think that having found you, I mean to let you go without first ascertaining where I might find you again?"

He's insane, was all she could think. How to escape? What to do? Humor him. Keep him calm until she could summon help.

"I see," she said in a smooth voice. "Very well, then . . . I am staying at the Bull Tavern. You may escort me there, if you like."

"At the Tavern? Never say so!" He frowned. Could it be that she was already spoken for? Had some sporting gentleman brought her along for additional entertainment? "Have a friend there, do you?" he asked lightly.

What to answer? One must remember, after all, that he was mad and anything might set him off. He didn't seem to like the thought of her having protection at the Bull. Perhaps she should generalize.

"A friend? Why, yes, one or two," she answered lightly.

He had noted her hesitation. What was this? His brow went up at her answer. "One or two? Don't you know?"

"As a matter of fact, I have two," she decided to tell him.

"Two?" He was in fact both surprised and just a bit shocked. She seemed such an innocent little thing; he had rather thought she was new to the profession she had taken on. It would appear that he was wrong. "Ah . . . do they know about each other?" his curiosity led him to inquire.

"Oh, yes," she answered easily. "They have been friends forever."

"And appear to be able to share their favorite possessions, no doubt."

Her nose wrinkled. "Oh, I don't know about that. Robby never likes Freddy to mount his hunter. Says he is hamhanded. . . ." She bit her lip. Had she said too much?

The tenth earl of Magdalen found himself momentarily bereft of speech. He looked over this stunning piece of fluff from head to foot and inquired, "Your . . . er . . . friend Robby won't share his hunter, but he will share you?"

She opened her dark eyes wide. What in thunder did this blade think? Suddenly she rather thought she knew and turned a deep shade of pink. Oh, for the love of . . . ! Never mind. Never mind. He was naught but an arrogant, conceited London rogue. Let him think what he would. She would never see him again!

"Share me?" she returned, her chin well up. "Oh, you mistake, sir. No one shares me . . . or owns me!"

They were fast approaching the inn, and she could see

17

her brother and Freddy in the courtyard. They appeared to be in a heated debate with yet another young man. She really didn't wish to enlighten this rogue any further as to her identity. What to do?

Robby looked up and discovered his sister being driven in one of the smartest phaetons he had ever clapped eyes on. The gentleman wielding the driving reins was someone he would only describe as a "top sawyer," a "blood," a Corinthian! Giving Freddy's sleeve a tug, he swore beneath his breath, for just such a man was *not* what Bell needed now. Another rogue to break her young heart? Devil!

The phaeton was brought to a halt, and Bell turned to her companion with a smile. "Thank you. . . . I must go." She turned and found Robby coming toward her. Quickly she alighted and was spared introductions when at that moment a shot rang out, and a group of intoxicated young men stumbled into the courtyard.

"Quick . . . we have to get Bell to her room!" snapped Robby, for indeed there appeared to be a brawl ensuing.

Freddy sighed and said, "But Robby . . . it's a mill. . . . You don't want to miss it, do you?"

"Damnation, Freddy, must get Bell away from here." Robby was already scurrying her past these men and up the back stairs.

"Right, then . . . let's put her away and hurry back," Freddy returned in a resigned fashion.

"Put me away?" Arabella retorted indignantly as her brother ushered her into her room. However, there was nothing else to do. Indeed, even Arabella saw that she couldn't venture outside with every gentleman in the place so neatly inebriated!

Chapter Four

Grosvesnor Square boasted some very fine houses and was a location much sought after by those members of the aristocracy desirous of leasing a fashionable situation for the London season. When he had ample time to survey his surroundings, Sir Robert Cullingham congratulated himself on putting his aunt Vi to the task of hiring a house for their stay in London.

"All the crack . . . this," commented Freddy as he glanced about the street and prepared to alight from the carriage. "Anyone can see that. Your aunt Vi is up to snuff, eh, Robby?"

"Whew," breathed Robby, calculating in his mind a season's cost for such an establishment, for it was obvious Vi had spared no expense. The town house was one of the finest in the square. "Lord, but Vi has gone and done it."

Arabella touched his coat sleeve in some concern. "Robby . . . is it too dear, do you think?"

He patted her gloved hand. "Probably, Sis, but no matter. The estate can well afford it, and *you* deserve it."

On their arrival, the front doors of Grosvesnor House were flung open by the servants. A woman of good height appeared, her arms opened wide to receive them. There was a joyful, genuine smile on her intriguing countenance. Violet Cullingham was not a particularly beautiful woman, yet she had an aura of grace and loveliness. Her fair, soft waves of gold were cut in the latest style and brushed away from her face. She was wearing her favorite jewels this morning, amethysts, and her highly styled gown was violet.

"Well!" she said by way of a welcome, and released a short, happy laugh. "You are finally here, and now we may begin!"

So it was for the next few days that under her aunt's guidance and at her aunt's side, Arabella was given a tour of the best of London. She would listen raptly to whatever *on-dits* her aunt chose to disclose to her. She would listen wide-eyed as her aunt gravely advised her that she must or must not do a particular thing. As it happened, on one morning their carriage passed an interesting avenue and Vi said, bringing Arabella's attention around, "Never, my love, ever find yourself walking down *this* street!"

Arabella looked at the fingerpost, which disclosed the name of the quiet avenue as Bow Street. "Why?" she inquired reasonably.

"My dear! It is where White's is located."

White's, as Arabella had already been advised on a previous occasion, was *the* most exclusive of the men's clubs in London. "What does that signify?" Arabella was a stickler for details.

"Why, there is a new window, a bow window, that has been installed. All the gentlemen stand at its pane and ogle whatever poor female is unwise enough to pass. It has ruined more than one young woman's reputation, let me tell you, so on no account must you pass through this avenue." She eyed her niece doubtfully. "Understand?"

Arabella glanced down the road and found nothing there of interest. Thus, with a shrug of her shoulder she allowed, "Very well."

Satisfied, the lady Violet proceeded to rattle on in her

fashion, giving various bits of interesting and very nearly scandalous gossip about the people they saw about town. Arabella was amused and, to some extent, even entertained by her aunt's frivolous conversation, but what she really wanted was to mount her mare and gallop through the lush green Hyde Park. This, she had been advised gravely by her aunt, was a "no, no." One never galloped through Hyde Park. It was not the thing.

Twenty minutes later, Arabella found herself the center-piece for a bevy of dressmakers all intent on pleasing the lady Vi, whose taste was not only elegant but demanding as well. Bell pulled one grimace after another as she was pushed, prodded, turned, and pinned. Her reflection in the looking glass was pleasing enough, but for a girl of Bell's restless disposition it was not enough compensation for the confinement.

At the end of this session, Arabella was shocked to hear her aunt say, "Burn it . . . or give it away if you must, but I never wish to see it again."

Arabella gasped, for her aunt was talking about the morning gown and spencer she had been wearing. While she knew it was not quite fashionable for London's *haute ton*, she couldn't bring herself to see it destroyed.

"Aunt Vi!" she objected.

"Hush, child," She clucked her tongue at Bell. "Only, do look at yourself." She turned her niece toward the look-ing glass.

Arabella could not help but see that the tight-fitting mint-green silk jacket with wide lapels of mint green satin and matching, form-fitting skirt were quite exceptional. She could see that the white lace ruffle of the high-necked blouse was a perfect complement to the outfit, as was the marvel-ous confection of mint-green feathers and silk pinned in her amber curls. Still, her morning gown and spencer had been newly purchased for her London sojourn. "Yes, but Vi . . ." she still tried to object.

21

"There. I am quite pleased with this morning's work," cut in her aunt airily. She turned to the seamstress and rattled off instructions for the remainder of their purchases before taking up her niece's hand, gloved in white lace, and saying, "Come along. We still must visit the milliners. . . ."

"Oh, Vi . . . no . . . not today . . ." Bell wailed helplessly. She was, however, given a short respite, for as they stepped outside, her aunt nearly bumped into the lady Jersey. The two women fell into an involved round of gossip, and, seeing her chance, Bell interjected lightly, "Dearest, you have a nice long chat with Lady Jersey. I am just going to go across to that quaint bookstore. I won't be long." With a charming smile thrown over her shoulder, she made her exit and crossed the busy street.

Bell was momentarily diverted from her purpose by a small urchin who held out a posy and hopefully indicated his wish to sell it. Arabella immediately smiled at the dirty child, put a coin in his hand, took up the violets, and turned, to bump directly into a tall, quite broad, and well-dressed gentleman. As she started to exclaim an apology, she looked up and recognized him as the one who had accosted her in Dorchester. She gasped and breathed on a scarcely audible note, "You!"

Shaun Standon, the tenth earl of Magdalen, inclined his head and admitted dryly, "No other, my love." He took up her elbow and directed her out of the way of passersby.

"Let go of me!" she demanded in outraged accents.

"Ah. Still under the protection of your two young men?" he teased.

"Of course. Could I have come to London otherwise?"

He looked her over and nodded with approval. "Very nice, sweetheart, and much more the thing." His eyes scanned provocatively the curves of her figure in her new walking ensemble.

She blushed hotly and started to pass him. He was surprised by her obvious confusion, by the color in her cheeks. What was this? He turned and moved along with her, saying lightly, "Where are we going?"

"*I*," said the lady pointedly, "am going to the bookstore. You, sir, should go on your way . . . or must I call for assistance?"

"Ah, I was forgetting. You have *two* gentlemen . . . ready to assist you at all times." He sighed in mock dismay. "Right, then, bring them on if you must."

She frowned at him. She could, of course, run to her aunt if he dared to take a liberty with her, but that was something she would do only as a last recourse. How devilishly humiliating that would be, especially with the lady Jersey on hand. No. She must just try and rid herself of him. She looked up at his face and discovered his blue eyes twinkling. That set her to blushing once more. "You must know they are not with me at the moment, but surely you don't mean to accost me in public." She pursed her lips and gave him an arch look.

"No, my love . . . not in public." He stopped her then by touching her hand, taking it to his lips, and looking down into her dark eyes. "So I will leave you to your own devices . . . *if* you promise to see me again."

"No," she returned sharply, but felt a certain attraction take hold of her.

"No? Then I am loath to quit your company now. In fact, I feel it incumbent upon me to remain as . . . er . . . protection for you until your young men take up the post again."

She stamped her foot at him, but she could see her aunt and the Jersey looking their way. Oh, no. What would the Jersey think? She was such a high stickler for the proprieties. She had to get rid of this dreadful rogue at once. "Oh, very well . . ." she conceded testily.

He grinned wickedly. "Tomorrow, then, at noon at the Red Lion in Soho."

She frowned, for she was quite sure this was a disreputable establishment, but she nodded anyway. After all, she didn't really have to go.

As though reading her thoughts, he added, "On your word of honor, madam?" His brow was raised.

"Would you take it?" she was momentarily surprised into replying.

"If you give it, yes, I would," he answered gravely. He was taking a chance, but she seemed so very serious over the matter, while he was merely amusing himself.

She sighed and resigned herself, "Oh, very well, then. On my word of honor." She was already devising a plan by which to protect herself from him on the morrow.

He tipped his beaver top hat to her, kissed her gloved fingers once more, and left her at the bookstore's door. However, Bell had not been in the store more than a moment when her aunt came upon her and demanded in a whisper, "My dearest love, my sweet angel, my delightful child, however did you manage to capture Magdalen's attention, and for all the world to see?"

Chapter Five

Magdalen! It was all she heard all the rest of the day. Shaun Standon tenth earl of Magdalen, was the wealthiest, handsomest, most sought after bachelor in all of London. There wasn't a match-making mama in town that didn't want him for her daughter. He was nearly thirty, her aunt said, and had no great liking for women. He was, however, a rake of some magnitude and broke hearts wherever he went.

Her aunt Vi had rattled on in this style, saying that he never showed any interest in marriageable chits and the one or two times that he had made this mistake, the poor girls in question languished with broken hearts.

Bell had blinked her eyes at this last and exclaimed, "Absurd! Over a man?" She shook her head. "*I* wouldn't do so. . . ." She thought fleetingly of the handsome soldier she had only recently been pining over and reiterated this statement forcefully, "It is a silly thing to do. One must pick oneself up and proceed. . . ."

Vi looked at her shrewdly, "As *you* are doing?"

Arabella's mobile eyebrow went up warningly. "Languish, indeed!" was all the response she meant to give on the subject.

"Yes, but I still don't know how you came to know Magdalen."

They had been relaxing over tea in the brightly furnished library, and it was at this juncture that Sir Robert and Freddy walked in unceremoniously, Freddy joining in the conversation with, "Magdalen? Bell knows Magdalen? Rubbish!"

Arabella leaned back against the yellow cushions of the sofa and eyed him haughtily. "Well, it isn't! I have met him, though what all this fuss is about, I can't fathom. I found his lordship both arrogant and rude!"

"Oh, you have taken him in dislike . . ." wailed Violet, and then, brightening, " . . . but he seemed to fancy you. . . ."

"Fancy m'sister?" struck in Sir Robert over his shoulder as he poured himself and his friend a glass of sherry. "Why on earth would a man like Magdalen fancy Bell?"

"Odious boy!" laughed Arabella. "What is that supposed to mean?"

"Well . . ."—Freddy coughed—"lovely girl, Bell . . . anyone can see that, but . . . well, Magdalen . . . you know . . ."

"What he means," clarified Robby, "is that Magdalen could have any woman he wanted. . . . And besides, how do you come to know him? It is impossible. Only seen him myself once since we've been in town, and *not* to talk to."

Three pairs of eyes waited for Arabella to respond to this very reasonable question. Her own eyes opened wide with the effort, but she managed "Oh . . . I startled his horses in Dorchester."

"You what?" asked three people at once.

"You know . . ." she returned impatiently, for she wanted the subject closed, " . . . near that little inn we stayed at in Dorchester where you and Freddy went to the cock fight. I was out walking. . . ."

"Which I didn't want you to do!" put in Robby with a frown.

"Yes, well, I startled his horses and . . . and he insisted

26

on seeing me to the inn. That was all. When I met him in town today, it was the merest thing . . . really."

"Yet he remembered you," said Vi thoughtfully.

"What does that signify?" returned Bella, blushing.

"Magdalen doesn't bother with young country girls unless . . ." said Vi, " . . . well, never mind that. You may depend upon it. You have caught his interest, my love."

"Nonsense." By this time Arabella was testy, and the subject was allowed to close. However, by the next morning she was carefully penning a letter and slipping it into a servant's possession, directing him to take it to Magdalen!

The tenth earl opened the scented envelope and raised an eyebrow to read.

My lord,
It is with sincere regret that I find I cannot keep our appointment at noon.
You will, I know, think poorly of me for not keeping my word, but then, it was forced from me, was it not?

Magdalen found himself disappointed to a degree that was not proportionate to the matter. Well, she had evidently discovered who he was, and he did not even have her first name. Very irritating, to be sure. How was he to find the chit again? He thought of her amber curls, her piquant face, and her dark eyes and felt his desires stirred, but being who he was, he then attempted to put her out of his mind and go about his business. This too, however, was suddenly thwarted by the arrival of yet another letter, and this one was brought by the post.

He recognized it at once—even before he broke the seal. It was from his uncle, Sir Jasper. With a resigned sigh, he unfolded the crisp note paper to read.

Shaun:

Honour me in this request, since you chose to ignore my previous requirement of you.

My ward, Rose Knoyles, should be arriving in London shortly and will be staying with Lady Violet Cullingham, who is a friend of yours, as I recall. It would please me greatly if I had your assurances that you will at least squire her about town on occasion.

Your uncle,
Jasper

With a curse, Magdalen threw the letter in the fire. His butler entered the study at this point and quietly inquired after his employer's needs, to which Magdalen replied scathingly, "Indeed, my needs are simple! To be left to my own devices!"

It was at this precise moment that the Cullingham butler, Thimes, opened the front door of the Cullingham town house and admitted a young woman of substantial height and elegant form. At first glance he could see that her traveling raiment was, though countrified, of superior quality and tasteful design. She held herself well, spoke with self-assurance, and immediately drew his respect in spite of the fact that her portmanteau was old and ragged and that no maid seemed to be in attendance. He nodded gravely when she gave him her name and asked to be taken to Lady Cullingham, for although her ladyship had neglected to mention the pending arrival of any such person, instinct guided him.

So it was that Arabella, in the middle of rapping Freddy soundly for some wayward remark, looked up and saw for the first time the girl whose future would soon be entwined with hers.

"Miss Rose Knoyles," announced Thimes properly before he quietly withdrew.

Lady Cullingham put down her cup of tea, turned, jumped to her feet, and, with her hands outstretched, went forward.

"Rose . . . why, my dearest child . . ." she exclaimed on a surprised but happy note. "Why . . . I was not expecting you for another week."

Rose blushed slightly as she found herself warmly embraced and said softly, "Oh, no. Jasper dispatched me with every assurance that you were expecting me. . . . I am so sorry . . ." She was frowning over the problem.

"Jasper," said Violet, clucking her tongue disparagingly but not adding anything to his name. She pinched Rose's cheek. "You must not fret. No, my dear. I received Jasper's letter only this morning, but if I am put out, it is only because I don't have your room in readiness, yet. You are *very* welcome." She turned to her family and said brightly, "Darlings, I want you to meet Sir Jasper's ward, Rose."

Arabella came forward at once and exclaimed merrily that she was very pleased to have another female in the house to thwart her dreadful brother and her odious Freddy. She looked up at this to notice, with some amusement, that Freddy was coloring up. Quickly she introduced the two young men to Rose and watched, for she could see they were both taken with her soft prettiness. Invited to relax and enjoy a cup of tea, Rose removed her chip bonnet and her kid gloves. Bella had the opportunity to look her over. She liked the young woman's eyes. They were fine and sharp and softly hazel in hue. Her hair was a short crop of tawny curls. Her figure was trim and youthful, and Bella put her down as much her own age, deciding in her fashion that she liked the newcomer!

And so the season began!

Chapter Six

Arabella couldn't sleep any longer. Two weeks had passed since Rose's arrival, and the two had become fast friends. So she got to her feet, slipped into her wrapper, and crossed the carpeted hall to Rose's bedchamber, where she knocked and then, without waiting for a reply, peeped in. As its hangings were drawn, the room was still encased in darkness, so she left the door open a crack and proceeded within.

Approaching the bed, Bella whispered, "Rose? Rose, are you asleep?"

"Yes. Go away."

"Come on, get up, do, and we'll go for a hack in Hyde Park. That's what we need, you know."

"What time is it?" inquired Rose in the voice of one groaning for life.

"Why . . . it is nearly seven o'clock. We can get in a good gallop before anyone sees . . ." suggested Arabella on a lively note.

"Sick. You are really sick," moaned Rose before turning and giving her friend her back.

"Does that mean you don't want to ride?" inquired Arabella, just a little dejected.

"Not only sick, but brilliant. Go back to bed, Bell. Vauxhall is tonight."

Arabella giggled in her fashion and left her friend to her sleep. It didn't take her long after that to throw on her riding habit, pat her amber curls into a semblance of order, and perch her black silk top hat rakishly onto those curls. This she took a moment over until she was satisfied with the effect, and then she was off to the stables. She could have, should have, waited for word to be sent around to the stables, which were a good distance from the house, but then a groom would have brought around her black and would have ridden at a discreet distance behind her. Arabella wanted her freedom. So she marched, crop in hand, as quickly as she could without running, nodded pleasantly to the surprised group of young grooms at the stable door, and took up her saddle.

Hurriedly, and in some horror, one of these grooms immediately ran forward to take the saddle from her and to assure her that he would have miss's horse ready in a thrice. Arabella laughed and informed him that she would attend to this office herself. As there was no stopping her, he stood back and watched in some awe as Arabella curried, brushed, and saddled her black gelding, led him out to the mounting block, and hoisted herself into the sidesaddle. She sighed over this, for she really wanted to ride astride, but that, she knew, was impossible in London. Now, if only she could ride in the park without anyone observing. Of course she could. It was early, too early for any of the fashionables to be on the strut yet!

The hour was certainly too early for London's fashionables, but already the streets were filling up with merchants transporting their wares. Hawkers were out, many of them only children, and the cry of "fresh bread," "fresh milk," and "pigeon tarts" could be heard above the clatter of horses' hooves.

In the midst of all this commotion was one urchin, a boy of less than ten years of age. He was on crutches, he was fair of face (what could be seen of it beneath the dirt), and he wielded a basket of hothouse flowers. His voice was feeble and did not carry as well as the other hawkers, so he thrust his basket out in an attempt to catch the interest of pedestrians.

Shaun Standon was tired from his night's pleasure of carousing with the boys. He had stayed in the company of one of his cyprian acquaintances, risen early, bathed, dressed, and left her still asleep to make his way home, where he was due to meet with his business agent. The boy caught the earl's eye and his sympathy, and he found himself crossing the busy avenue, wielding his nervous gray through the hubbub to generously fling a coin at the lad.

The urchin smiled gratefully, but as the gentleman then began to move off, he cried out fretfully, "Eh . . . sir . . . yer flowers. . . ?" He wasn't a beggar and would have this understood. Shaun Standon, tenth earl of Magdalen, saw this at once, thanked the boy, and took up a posy of violets. A moment later he was riding off and feeling a fool, holding the posy in his tight grasp. With a grimace he thanked the fates that no one was about to observe him!

"Well, Cricket, my black, no one is about, no one is looking, and we are going to fly . . ." breathed Arabella as she spurred her horse into a canter and took the bridle path across the park. The path ran along the lovely serpentine and Bell gave her horse his head, laughing pleasurably as he kicked off some of his fidgets and took to the wind. It was a lovely morning. Flowers were in bright array, swans floated gracefully in the serpentine, and Arabella felt that suddenly all was well with the world. She had been needing this run, and therefore made no effort to check her gelding as he flew down the path. She didn't try to keep him to the path when he chose to fork off to another narrower one, which led into a woodland landscape. It was all too wonderful to feel his power beneath her, to be a part of his enthusiasm for life.

Meanwhile, Shaun Standon pulled a face and hurriedly turned his dapple gray into the park to avoid one of Prinny's cohorts, for that particular individual would be sure to poke as much fun as he could over the flowers. At any rate, Shaun told himself, he could take the shortcut through the wooded park. It was at this juncture that he slowed to a jog, for he was rounding the narrow bend.

Cricket heard, sensed, that something was ahead, something was all too near, and he brought himself to a sudden halt. His abrupt stop nearly unseated Arabella, and she found herself bouncing out of her sidesaddle. An all-too-familiar man's voice brought her eyes up with a snap, and she found herself staring at the tenth earl of Magdalen.

"We are served now tit for tat, beloved," he drawled in an amused tone. "But pleased as I am to have found you at last, tell me, minx. What are you doing racing through the park at this early hour?"

Up went her chin. "It is because of the hour that I am . . . er, racing through the park." Then in her candid manner she confided, "Cricket and I have been missing the open fields, and we both needed a good run."

He found her disarmingly charming, and he laughed as he reached over and flicked her nose. "Oh, sweetheart, I don't mean to let you escape me this time."

She found that his touch, casual as it was, stirred her. She knew her cheeks were flooded with color, and quickly she sought a reply.

"I think, my lord, that choice is not yours," she managed.

"Oh?" he returned, his brow up, his eyes unreadable. He remembered the flowers he held and with an inclination of his head he presented them to her. "These, my minx, are for you."

She was surprised into a giggle. "What is this? Always

the ready 'Don Juan,' my lord? I was told you are the Prince of Rakes, and now I am convinced this was no exaggerated tale. But why do you bother with me? Haven't you enough hearts in your collection?''

His eyes flickered meaningfully, and his tone was low and seductive. "Perhaps it is not your heart I am after.''

She frowned and tilted her head—much like a sparrow—over these words. Dawning lit in her dark eyes and shocked any and all possible responses out of her head. All she could think was, How dare he! Why, the man was an arrogant boor! She threw the posy of flowers to the wind, turned her horse, and broke all rules by galloping and cutting across the park's green lawns. She was risking total censure, but she wasn't thinking.

He was surprised and did not follow her. Why, she was behaving like an outraged lady of quality when all she was . . . well, after all, she was another man's mistress. This was all very confusing. She was no innocent, yet she had behaved as though he had offered her insult—and it wasn't an act, for the blush in her cheeks had been quite real. What was this?

She traveled with two young bucks and openly admitted the fact. She wandered about London unattended and was, therefore, subject to the proposal he had just given her. Why, then, had she run? Certainly this was a mystery. First thing after business he was going to search out this woman, for he had quite made up his mind: this cyprian was going to be his!

Chapter Seven

Freddy Eastdean had discovered in Rose Knoyles the dream he had always pursued. From the moment of their meeting, he had declared himself her obedient servant, her humble slave, and her gallant knight. His hazel eyes followed her every move in gentle (if absurd) worship, faltering only when challenged by his dearest and closest friend. This because Sir Robert Cullingham felt much the same about Rose.

Thus, the weeks had been fraught with their rivalry, much to the amusement of both Arabella and Vi. This night, with Vauxhall full to overflowing, found them at each other's throats in their attempts to win the lady's attention.

"Walk with me, Rose . . . now, before Robby notices that we are gone . . ." whispered Freddy in her ear.

She smiled gently at him and chided, "But Freddy . . . Robby comes now, and with my negus."

Freddy pouted, and Robert, who had by this time reached their side, gallantly offered, "Your refreshment, my lovely."

She thanked him and gracefully sipped. Freddy did not wish to give up, however, and made yet another attempt. "Come on, Rose. I will show you that fountain you admired earlier."

"Rose will do better in our box watching those jugglers. . . . Look, Rose . . . there!" stuck in Sir Robert.

"Yes, they are wonderful," agreed Rose with a bemused smile. She liked both Sir Robert and Freddy, but it was a bit tiring, forever having to "handle" their rivalry. She looked about for Arabella and, without really thinking, remarked, "I wonder where Bell can have gone off to." No sooner was the question out than it was regretted.

Sir Robert's brows drew together in a frown. "Deuce take it!" he ejaculated after scanning their immediate surroundings. The place was inundated with fashionables, most of them good acquaintants, but nowhere could he see either his aunt Violet or Arabella. "Where can they have gone off to?"

Rose attempted to repair the damage. "No doubt Vi has bumped into an old friend and poor Bell is stuck in polite conversation."

Arabella's brother grinned at the thought. "Not she, the little devil. No doubt that if that is what happened, my Bell found the first chance while they were talking to slip off for an adventure." He started off but Rose held his wrist.

"Stay, Robby. . . . Give Arabella another moment or two. . . ."

He thought this over. Vauxhall was a riotous place filled with individuals determined to find hedonistic pleasures. True, they were in elegant surroundings, away from most of the sporting lads, but even so, he didn't like to think of Arabella wandering about alone in Vauxhall. "Well . . ." he allowed reluctantly, "perhaps for another moment or two."

"Look, there . . ." said Rose, attempting to capture his attention once more. "Who is that man? Is he the Beau I have heard so much about?"

"Lord, yes. That is Beau Brummell," answered Freddy in her ear. "There isn't a dandy in all of England that doesn't ape his style."

36

"Really? But he doesn't look a dandy," answered Rose on a note of surprise. "In fact . . . I quite approve of his dress."

"Why," responded Sir Robert in some shock, "I should think so! Rose, my dearest, he is Beau Brummell!"

This was a statement that Rose insisted he explain, and as the two young men attempted to put into adequate words the admiration in which their fellow Englishmen held the Beau, Arabella was enjoying the sights immensely.

Never before had she been to such a fairy-tale land. There were torch lights burning everywhere. There were gaslights of various shapes and sizes. There were crystals, flowers, ponds, fountains, music, and tiny walk bridges over ornamental streams. It was enough to hold a girl like Arabella spellbound for several minutes. She had indeed been forced into social amenities with one of her aunt's old dowager friends, but then, while the two of them were deep in conversation, Bell made her escape just as Sir Robert had surmised, slipping away unnoticed.

She had gone further than she had intended, and when a group of young men bent on drinking themselves into bliss met her gaze, she was sure she should return to the protection of her brother. However, as she backed away from this scene, a familiar male voice sent a shiver through her, and a strong male hand took hold of her shoulder. She could feel his grip through his gloves and through the satin of her black cloak. She spun around sharply, to find Shaun Standon looking down at her. Oh, such blue eyes! It was her first discernible thought before she discovered that her body and then her cheeks were on fire.

Her cloak had slipped away from her shoulder as she moved, revealing her lovely white skin and the softness of her yellow silk gown. His blue eyes glinted in appreciation, and he could not help but realize that she ignited a sure passion in him. She was certainly a charmer, with her amber curls framing her piquant face and her cherry lips pursed in surprise.

"Hallo, my love . . ." he whispered softly, and began taking her down a narrow walk path.

Vauxhall was filled with many such paths, and nearly all of them were designed with lovers in mind. It was a place meant for soft seduction, and Shaun Standon meant to put it to use.

"Where are you taking me?" she demanded at once.

"Where we were destined to go from the first moment of our meeting," he answered without hesitation. He looked around the bend of the evergreen maze, and, finding there a secluded spot, he pulled her gently, easily into its folds.

She could have stopped him. She could have yanked out of his hold and run. She could have resisted before, when they were still in the open, surrounded by people. She could have . . . but she didn't. He was taking her into his arms; he was bending to brush his lips against hers. She knew it, and she allowed it—nay, she asked for it—as her hands wrapped around his neck and her supple body pressed against him.

His mouth closed on hers, taking her lips in gentle sweetness, parting them in arrogant self-assurance, burning them with his own overwhelming desire. Damn, but he wanted her, had been wanting her for some weeks, and now that he had her, he wasn't about to waste his time!

She yielded to his kiss, discovering that it was something she wanted. He was a rake. She heard the voice inside her mind warning. Run, Arabella, run. Insanely she answered herself by responding to his kiss and giving him yet another. He was a rakehell, and she meant to learn from him, not be caught by him! She would tease him, flirt with him, bring him to a point, and then she would freely (and with her heart still intact) walk away!

She had learned her lesson when she was just a green

girl in the country falling in love with a faithless officer. She had seen how a man could kiss and run without a backward glance. Experience was all she needed. She would get her experience from this Prince of Rogues! When she was through, no man would ever hurt her again!

His hands started to take more than she was willing to give, and as he shifted his hold and brought his palm to her breast, she broke away and said on a breathless note, "I must go. . . ."

He frowned, thinking she must be here with her gentlemen friends, and called after her retreating form, *"Your name . . . ?"*

She giggled, turned to look at him, and called back, "Arabella," then hurried off and out of his view. She had to get back to her box before her brother and Violet knew what she was about. Well, well, Arabella, she told herself. You have had a fine lesson indeed. You have kissed the Earl of Magdalen, breaker of hearts, and you have walked away still your own woman! A doubt needled her. Bell . . . you wanted to kiss him because he was attractive. She answered immediately, What is in that, pray, but a natural and healthy desire. A woman shouldn't want to kiss a man she doesn't find attractive, after all! Wasn't she smarter now than she had been when she was hurt in the country? She would flirt, dally, and tease with the best of them, but never again would she give her heart! Prince of Rakes, indeed!

Chapter Eight

"Why do you look like that?" Arabella inquired of her friend as the hackney coach took them across town to their destination. "I thought you wanted to go."

Rose nearly crossed her eyes in her attempt to express what she was feeling, and her voice came out in squeaking tones, "I do. I did. I am going. . . ."

"Then why do you look ready . . . to be sick?" pursued Arabella with a giggle.

"Because I am going to be sick," replied Rose at once.

Arabella released a series of giggles and, putting her hand over her cherry lips, replied, "Yes . . . it is terribly exciting, isn't it?"

"Tell me again how we shall breeze through this and not get caught," returned Rose prosaically.

"Oh, my Rose, I am persuaded you are not as poor-spirited as you put on. Now, you know you want to attend this bazaar as much as I do, and since Sir Robert and Freddy were so disobliging as to go out of town for that miserable Alvanley and his miserable speech . . . well, then we didn't have a choice. Today is the last day. If we don't go today, we won't have a chance till next year, and next year . . . why, who can say where we will be then?"

"Yes, that sounds reasonable, but I don't understand

why the men went to Alvanley's. They told me just the other day he is a detestable Tory."

"Hmmm. Want to know what the opposition is up to, I suppose. Robby is always very thorough in everything he does. He is a Whig, wants to play in Parliament, so nothing for it but to dive in wholeheartedly. And what Robby does, Freddy takes up. That's the way it has always been."

"Hmm. Even with women?" inquired Rose thoughtfully.

Arabella eyed her. "Ah, that is something else. My brother and Freddy have never wanted the same woman before. In fact, I have never seen Freddy interested, really interested, in a female before." She laughed freely. "Which one do you mean to have?"

Rose sighed. "I am afraid my heart isn't in it. I don't really want either of them."

"I didn't think so." Then a brightly-colored tent in the distance caught her eye, and she tugged at the blue silk of her friend's tailored spencer. "Look . . . isn't that grand?"

"Hmmm . . . you don't think Vi will find out we didn't go to the dressmaker, do you?"

"Doesn't matter. When we get back, we'll tell her we didn't go there. . . . Oh, Rose, look at that horse. Isn't he famous?"

"I don't like him. Too much flash. What do you mean, we will tell her we didn't go there?"

"Mean to tell her the truth after we have had our adventure. It is so much easier that way. Take my punishment."

"Oh, God," cried Rose. "I don't want to take your punishment."

Arabella laughed. "You won't have to. It was my plan; it will be my punishment."

"Never you mind. We are both in it."

"Right. So we will both—"

"Do shut up, Bell," cut in her friend caustically.

It didn't take them long after they arrived at the fair to

find the fortune teller. They entered and found a gypsy woman who took first Arabella's hand, whipped off her glove, and said that only the Tarot cards would do.

Rose had always been enthralled with this sort of thing and took great interest in the reading of the cards. When her turn arrived, she asked a great many questions concerning the interpretation of the cards. Finally the gypsy offered to give her a lesson for a price. Rose quickly put her coins on the table.

Arabella laughed and said she'd had enough of fortune telling for one morning and wanted to visit the cage reputed to hold the two-headed calf.

"You disgusting girl," said Rose. "But should you wander off alone, Bell?"

"It is the tent adjacent to this. I won't be far." Bell tripped off happily as she left her friend to the mysteries of Tarot.

The earl of Magdalen did not often attend fairs and their like. He had wearied of such affairs many years ago. However, he was an avid boxing fan, as were his closest cronies, and on this, the last day of the fair, a major boxing match had been held. He and a few of his friends had risen early and made their way to the big tent for one of the finest matches the earl had seen in some time. The match was over, and as the earl stepped out of the tent, he laughed with a friend and then went stock still as he watched a pretty little amber-haired thing in a fashionable ensemble of the palest green skip across the dirt path from the fortune teller's to the animal tent.

His friend shook his shoulder and frowned. "Shaun . . . don't you hear me, man? We are going across town to Bull Tavern. Come, have a bumper of ale with us before you sit with your man . . ." he urged, for the earl was promised to his man of business for the remainder of the afternoon.

"What . . . oh . . . no . . . Buzz . . . you go on. . . ." He started off after the girl in green, his thoughts bumping one another in a mad rush. She was here. She seemed to be alone. She was lovely, sprightly, desirable. He had to have her, and this time he would make an assignation with her that she must keep!

Arabella happily paid her ha'penny, entered the tent, took one look at the pathetic creature, and nearly sobbed. A moment later she was rushing out of the tent, upset with herself for having gone to gawk at the poor sickly creature. She bumped right into the earl's hard, lean body and looked up to find his glistening blue eyes. "Oh . . ." was all she managed to say.

He laughed and pulled her along, taking her to an empty aisle between the two tents. "Wasn't the two-headed calf to your liking?" he teased, for he could see that she was upset.

"Poor thing . . ." was what she responded. "And . . . they don't feed it enough. . . . My lord . . . couldn't we do something?"

"They feed it. They have to. It earns their keep," he returned softly, and touched her chin. Then immediately he brought the subject around to his interests. "And so your name is Arabella?"

"Yes," she peeped at him, "and yours. . . ?"

"I know that you know my name, my full name. Why not tell me your full name?"

"No," she returned simply. "That would not do."

He laughed. "Wouldn't it? I am afraid I can't agree."

"Ah, but that is because we have different ends in mind."

"Do we? I think I cannot agree with you there either."

She laughed. "Arrogant blade. Now let me go. I have a friend waiting for me in the fortune teller's tent. She will wonder where I have gone off to."

43

"She?" And in some puzzlement, "You are here alone with another female? How is this?"

"We told a fib and escaped for the morning. . . ." She frowned. "Do you know the time?"

"Indeed, my minx, it is nearly noon."

She gasped, "I can't believe it. We have hardly seen anything yet and must return by one o'clock. Drat!"

He laughed again, enjoying himself immensely. "Then allow me to give you and your friend escort on the fairgrounds before I see you both home safely."

She dimpled flirtatiously, "Oh . . . I can't do that, my lord."

"And why not?" His fine, dark brow was up; his eyes surveyed her face for a clue.

"Oh . . . well, as to that . . . it just wouldn't do . . ." she said by way of a vague explanation as she tried to think how to get out of this one.

"It would do a great deal more than allowing you to wander about alone." He touched her chin with one finger, uplifting it, and said softly, "Don't you realize what a delectable morsel you are . . . and what danger that puts you in?"

She glittered with amusement, "Hmmm . . . you, my lord, are making me all too aware . . . of what danger I am in."

He chuckled and this time held her chin in some show of affection. "Little she-devil, you *do* make my blood run."

She wanted the game to continue. He had, from the moment they first met, treated her like some town cyprian. She couldn't imagine why he thought that of her, but apparently he did, and she was amusing herself by allowing him to believe this. However, she would have to be careful. "Run . . . yes, I must, and no . . . you may not give me escort. I have reasons why I dare not be seen with you."

When he touched her shoulders and bent to drop a light kiss upon her cherry lips, he was startled to feel a charge of excitement race through him. Damn, he thought, it was just a nothing kiss, yet full with such power! "Do you?" he asked huskily. "But I have excellent reasons to want you to be seen with me on my arm . . . *in* my arms. . . ." His tone was seductive, provocative.

In spite of all her resolutions, she found herself very nearly falling under the spell of his deep blue eyes. She caught herself and managed a naughty reply much in keeping with his style. "Oh, my handsome lord, when I go into *your* arms, it won't be for show. . . ." She steeled herself against him. Think, Arabella, she said in way of splashing cold water on her face, think about the gall of the man. Yes, she answered, he is dreadful. But oh, how her body tingled. Stop, Arabella! Think about his arrogance! Yes, of course, his arrogance.

"Minx!" he said with a soft laugh, "*only* come into my arms." He was feeling all too attracted to the amber-haired chit.

"Perhaps," she returned playfully, "but for now . . . I *must* go."

"Meet me tomorrow, then?" he asked intently.

"I would love to, my lord, but I am committed elsewhere."

"Then the next day," he responded immediately.

"If I can, I will send you word." She ran out of his reach then and dived around the bend in the aisle, waiting only until she could see him walk in the opposite direction. "Whew," she breathed out loud, and ducked into the fortune teller's tent.

"Rose!" cried Arabella, peeping around the opening in the tent and watching him walk away and out of sight. "Rose, aren't you done yet?"

"Hmmm . . ." said Rose, looking up from the cards. "Yes, sorry, Bell . . . but these are fascinating."

"Good . . . but we have to go soon and have hardly seen a thing. Come along. . . . I need to talk to you." She hadn't yet confided in Rose about her encounters with the earl of Magdalen, but the time had come to seek her friend's opinion. She felt herself in waters that were just a touch deep. Sooner or later he would find out who she was, and then he could hurt her reputation if he so chose. This was the fear that had suddenly occurred to her and now had to be discussed!

Chapter Nine

"My lord . . ." Jeffrey, Magdalen's man of business, stood patiently, waiting for his lordship's attention to return to the matters at hand.

The earl played absently with his lower lip, evidently disinterested and bored with the affairs of his estate. His mind was filled with the image of an amber-haired minx with dark sassy eyes and full cherry lips.

"There is the Cullingham ball. We must send our response, you see. . . ."

The earl frowned, but his blue eyes clicked to attention when he put out his hand for Violet Cullingham's invitation and read it once more. She was giving a ball in honor of her niece, Arabella Cullingham, and her dear friend's ward, Rose Knoyles. If he found it interesting that the name Arabella should plague him at all turns, he put this aside and would not allow it to affect his decision regarding another dull ball. However, the invitation was from Vi, whom he respected, and then too, it was for Rose, whom he cared about. He hadn't even found the time to pay her a morning call as yet, so he answered his man in the affirmative, asking him to remind him about the affair as it drew near.

"There is also the matter of your agent at Salisbury Estate, my lord. He is not well liked, and I fear there is good cause. . . ."

"Then you think I must travel to Salisbury?" sighed the Earl.

"I think the matter needs your personal attention," replied Jeffrey cautiously.

"Right then, I will leave within the next couple of days and not be back in town until the weekend." He frowned. Would this put a spoke in his designs for Arabella? Would she send a note? Ah, well, it couldn't be helped! What would be would be.

Arabella was with Rose in her bedchamber at that very moment, her dark eyes wide as Rose informed her of her long-standing acquaintance with the Prince of Rakehells!

"You mean your guardian . . . actually requested the earl to offer for you?" Arabella squeaked. "How dreadful for you . . . for the earl. . . ."

"That is putting it mildly, for you must know that the earl refused and walked out in something of a temper, and Bell . . . I learned afterward from one of the servants that my doting guardian, dearest Jasper, actually threatened Shaun. He told him that he would cut me off without a sou if he did not offer for me," said Rose with some indignation as she recalled the incident.

"I can't believe it."

"Well, believe it."

"Then what happened?" Bell's eyes were still wide.

"Jasper likes to get his own way, you see. He thought that if he sent me to Vi, I would be put in the earl's way, and perhaps something might come of it."

"Yes, but does he mean to leave you out of his will as he threatened if nothing does come of it?"

Rose smiled. "He is—in my case, at least—all bark, you know, and very little bite."

"But does the earl know you are in town?"

"I suppose. Jasper did say he would write to inform him of it."

"Then . . . he is the rudest man imaginable!" said Arabella in some irritation. "How dare he not pay you a morning call! After all, you are friends. It is the least he could do."

"No, Bell, you don't understand. Shaun probably feels that Vi Cullingham is capable enough of showing me around London, and he doesn't wish to encourage Jasper by paying any attention to me. No doubt that has kept him away."

"I see . . ." said Arabella thoughtfully. "What about the ball? Vi tells me he has not yet responded. Do you think he will stay away?"

Rose shrugged. "With Shaun one can never tell."

They were interrupted at that moment by a knock on the door. Rose called out lightly, absently, for her mind was still on their discussion, "Come in."

The door opened, and Arabella's brother stuck in his handsome head and said brightly, "Come on downstairs, do. . . . Bell, there is someone here you will want to see."

Arabella looked up with some interest, for she knew her brother well enough to see that he was highly elated. As this was not in keeping with his usual placidity, she moved with a certain measure of curiosity. "*Who* is here?" she demanded at once as she got to her feet.

"Come and see" was the tease he threw at her before he turned and hurried off to return to their guest.

She looked at Rose. "I wonder who it can be."

Practical as ever, Rose moved toward her door and invited, "Shall we go and see?"

Mr. James Huxley stood a good six feet tall. He was well built in a slender and angular style. His ash blond hair fell in layered waves to his neck and framed a pleasantly lean face that became quite boyishly handsome when he smiled. His eyes were pale blue behind metal-framed spectacles. His dress for town was fashionable enough, but still he had the air of a man unconcerned with such fripperies. He certainly did without fobs and dandy airs.

The Huxley ancestral home and estates bordered Cullingham Grange, and he was wont to spend many a pleasant day in the company of the Cullinghams. He was Sir Robby's senior by two years and had therefore graduated from Cambridge before Robby and Freddy. Upon completion of James's studies, his father (and only living parent) had decided it was time his eldest son went abroad. James had found his eyebrow twitching, for he was a young man with a will of his own; however, he did want to travel, so in spite of his father's command, he obeyed. He found he enjoyed traveling so much he did not wish to return home. He was called to return on several occasions, for the old Squire Huxley was yet another who would have his own way. James managed to stay out of reach and abroad for an additional year; however, his father began to bring pressures to bear upon him, and so he returned. Had he known what was in store for him, he would not have done so.

The squire had sat him down as soon as he stepped through the doors of his home and quickly, boldly told James what was expected of him as the heir apparent. Marriage. Indeed, marriage to Maria Yardley—and it was to take place at once. James laughed and said he would not do it. The squire then recounted all the duties of an heir. All the duties he owed his sisters, his younger brother. You see, Maria Yardley's fortune was considerable. James was independent, he was willful, and he certainly had a mind of his own, but he also felt a tremendous sense of responsibility to his name and his family. In the end he accepted, and the banns were posted.

He was recounting part of this tale into Robby's and Freddy's ears when Rose and Arabella entered the library.

"Jimmy!" shrieked Arabella with glee as she skipped across the room and flung herself at Mr. Huxley.

"Hallo, little one." Mr. Huxley received her just as warmly, and without the least bit of ceremony. He was a good five years her senior and had from their earliest meeting taken her on as something of a pet. He had her well off the ground, but when he saw a fair young woman at Arabella's back, he set her down and flicked her nose. "You are a sight for sore eyes."

She rapped his arm playfully and pouted. "Am I? Well, you certainly stayed away long enough. Oh, James . . . your last letter was more than four months ago."

"Yes, but I did write." He grinned.

"So you did," she conceded with a sigh, and took up his ungloved hand. She had for many years admired him beyond friendship. There had even been a time when she had had a daydream or two about him, though friendship often precludes such thoughts. She turned to her friend and noticed that Rose seemed most interested in this newcomer. "Jimmy . . . I want you to meet someone. This is Miss Rose Knoyles. She is Sir Jasper Standon's ward and Vi's friend and is staying here with us." She turned to Rose. "And this is our dearest Jimmy Huxley. His father is Squire Huxley, and their estate borders ours." Thus satisfied that the amenities had been observed, she folded her hands together and said, "There. Now let us sit and be comfortable while Jimmy tells us everything!"

Sir Robby laughed and pronounced his sister a minx without reserve but said that indeed, they did want to hear all about Jimmy's travels. Freddy agreed that this was so, slapped James on the shoulder, and told him that Greece was a place he had always wanted to visit.

Robby frowned. "That's not true. You never wanted to go to Greece until you met Byron last week and he got you started on the subject."

"Well, as to that . . ." Freddy began to defend his position.

"Oh, stop!" laughed Arabella as she plopped herself on

51

the sofa and motioned for James to be seated. "Come on, Jimmy. You sit here, across from Rose and me. . . . Freddy, we will hear all about Greece presently, but there is something that I need to know."

"Oh?" said James as the question had been directed at him, "What is that?"

"Some months ago I happened to meet your father while I was out riding, and he wanted to know if I would have you."

"What?" It was nearly a shout. "Never say father dared. . . !"

She giggled. "He is a dear, and I have never minded his very odd manners. Besides, it was most flattering. Said he preferred me over Maria Yardley."

At this both Freddy and Robby choked, and Freddy said, "Egad, I should think so! Maria Yardley is . . . is . . ."

Before he was able to put his opinion of Maria Yardley into words, Jimmy interrupted softly, " . . . is a lovely young woman and has consented to be my wife."

This had the effect of silencing the room. It was so quiet that Freddy was sure he could hear his thoughts out loud and wondered with a sick feeling if anyone else could as well. Of course it was Arabella that spoke first and with a question she couldn't contain.

"*You* are going to marry . . . Maria Yardley?" And then again out of control, "But . . . James . . . not *you*!" She was fairly certain that his affections had never been attached to Maria. Why, then, was he marrying the girl if not to gain her vast fortune? The thought that her dear Jimmy was making a marriage of convenience rather disgusted her, and she could not help but show this by her expression.

He did not take offense. He knew her too well and merely released a rueful laugh, saying softly, "Don't think too poorly of me, Bell."

"No . . . no . . . but James . . . why?" she wailed.

He glanced in Rose's direction. These were dear friends, and he was not adverse to discussing his future with them, especially since he wanted Robby for his best man. However, Rose was a stranger to him. Arabella saw this at once and clucked her tongue. "Never mind Rosey," she said easily. "You may count her one of us, and besides, whatever you tell me is going to end in her ears anyway, for I have lately found myself in the habit of telling her everything that enters my head."

Rose chided her, "Arabella, Mr. Huxley may not want his private affairs taken abroad."

Arabella conceded this with a wave of her hand. "No, of course he does not, and you won't spread about anything he says, right?"

"No, no, of course I would not, but . . ."

"Then it is all settled," summed up Arabella in her fashion. "Go on, James, tell us now, if you please: why are you marrying Maria and not me?" She dimpled on the question in a style all her own.

He chuckled. "Brat. That is all your fault, and well you know it. You convinced my father that you wouldn't have me, and he turned to Miss Yardley instead."

"What a horribly lowering thought," said Arabella, pulling a face.

"No, my girl. It is something in your favor that he considered you at all," laughed James wickedly.

"Well, really, James, that is doing it rather too brown, if you please," retorted Arabella, putting up her chin in playful annoyance.

He smiled. "Well, you don't have the lands to offer the Huxley name, and yours is a modest inheritance; however, he has always been fond of you and thought I might take to the idea of marriage if you were the bride."

"Ah . . . but you *did* take to the idea of marriage," she pursued. "I was made to see where my duties lie—" James returned softly.

"Yes, but James . . ." interrupted Robby at this, ". . . your father isn't in debt. I mean, there is no need for you to take such a step. . . ."

"It seems the Yardley family is anxious for the match . . . and have dangled some very advantageous marriage settlements before my father's eyes." He stopped and frowned, thinking perhaps he was being unfair in stating this about his parent.

"Go on," prompted Arabella. "Such as . . . ?"

"Such as a situation for my brother. He will be ordained at the end of this season, and as it happens they are in a position to offer him a modest parish."

"Stop! I can't believe Jeffrey would allow you to sacrifice yourself just to . . ."

"He doesn't know. I purposely forbade Father from telling him anything yet."

"Yes, but surely . . ." struck in Freddy, aghast that his friend was marrying a young woman whom he personally found unattractive both in looks and personality. "You can't mean to marry just to set up your brother!"

"He is my younger brother, and therefore it is my duty to see to his future."

"No, it is not. That is your father's duty," returned Arabella, "which he is sidestepping by using you!"

"And then there are my sisters. They are pets—you know they are—and will soon be needing their seasons in London. Whatever you may say, it is my duty as heir to take a bride and see to their futures. . . ."

"Duty, duty, duty!" said Arabella in some disgust. "This makes me ill. You have forgotten the word 'love.' "

James did not look at her. "I am not attached elsewhere," he said, and then with a smile, "This seems the best solution."

"Ay, the easiest," put in Freddy in a voice of doom, "but not the happiest."

There was a moment of quiet after this pronouncement,

and Rose broke it gently with, "It seems to me that as Mr. Huxley's friends, you should be wishing him well, not depressing him."

Arabella giggled and said to James, "You see, she is ever so smart, and practical."

Rose's statement brought both Robby and Freddy to a sense of etiquette, and they stepped forward to offer their felicitations. Arabella, however, withheld hers for a moment, studying Jimmy and this new situation in some concern. She had to get him out of this predicament, but how? It occurred to her that if he had just become engaged, he should still be with his new fianceé.

At the first opportunity she managed yet another question: "But then, James . . . if you are engaged to marry Miss Yardley, what are you doing in London?"

"Ah, her parents decided that we should take up residence at their London town house, where they mean to launch us into society with an elaborate engagement ball."

"I see," said Arabella slowly. "When is this expected to be?"

"As it happens, not for another month. The family is still in mourning over Maria's late aunt. The year of mourning will end on the twentieth of next month. Why?"

"Oh, I was just wondering how much time . . . I mean . . . whether or not Rose and I have enough time to select our gowns for the event . . . assuming we will be invited." She smiled sweetly.

"Naughty puss, of course you will be invited," he answered at once, but he glanced at her and wondered what she had in mind.

"Then I wish you joy, and, if it is in my power, to make certain you shall have it. . . ." She turned to Rose. "There, Rosey, have I wished him happy to your liking?"

Rose eyed her, and a doubt flickered in her quick mind about Bell's sincerity, but she responded quietly,

"Hmmm." She turned to James and extended her hand. "And I, Mr. Huxley, wish you much happiness."

He took up her hand and lightly kissed her fingertips, but as he released them, his pale blue eyes found the gold flecks in her hazel ones and lingered there a moment before he turned to answer a jocular remark of Freddy's.

Chapter Ten

The Cullingham coach rumbled along the busy streets of London as its driver neatly wielded his team through the thick of traffic. Within, two smartly dressed young ladies were too deep in conversation to take note of the passing scenes.

"Come on, Rosey. . . . Why such a face?" Arabella eyed her friend a moment. "There is no need for you to be shy," she sighed. "It is a pity, of course, that Vi couldn't accompany us this morning, but what does that signify? It is perfectly correct for us to be paying this morning call."

"Is it? Then why didn't you wish me to mention it to your brother? And why not mention it to Mr. Huxley?"

"Oh, I do wish you would stop calling him Mr. Huxley!" said Arabella on a note of exasperation. "His name is James, and as he is staying with us for the time being, you might as well get used to using his first name." Then, after a pause and a sly look her way, "After all, I noticed he used your first name by the close of the evening. . . ." With this she giggled.

"Never mind turning away from the question. I will have my answer," said Rose calmly, though some color had come into her cheeks.

"I did not wish to tell Robby, for he would think I am

up to some mischief, and I did not wish to tell James, for he might have felt it his deuced 'duty' to join us in this visit.''

''What would have been the harm in that?'' Rose's brows were up with the query.

''Silly chit,'' chided Arabella amicably, ''you know that the boys are off this morning hunting down a lodging for him. While it is all very well for him to stay with us for a short time, he must be established for the season, and it is already quite late for him to find something decent.'' Again she eyed her friend quizzically. ''Or would you prefer he stayed with us for the season?''

''Certainly not!'' snapped Rose.

''Oh? Why not? Don't you like poor James?'' Bell inquired in all innocence.

''Don't be nonsensical. That is not what I mean.''

''Ah, I did think that you had started to . . . find him interesting,'' said Bell lightly, and then added, ''I am so glad the boys insisted he leave his hotel and stay with us. It will be such fun.''

''Tell me again why we are paying this morning call to a girl you not only dislike but disapprove of as well.''

''Oh, I only disapprove of her as a match for James,'' returned Arabella.

''Then you do not dislike her?'' Rose pursued challengingly.

''Oh, as to that . . . perhaps I never really gave her a chance. We shall do that this morning,'' was all the reply Arabella meant to give on this score. The coach was slowing to a halt, and Arabella looked out its open window and observed, ''Ah, Kensington Place. Quite lovely.''

Rose eyed her warily but offered no comment beyond a soft grunt.

Some moments later they were taken to a richly appointed parlor decorated in the first stare of elegance and told by the butler that ''Miss'' would be in to visit with them directly. They were kept waiting there some ten minutes before "Miss" finally appeared. Arabella's temper was on the rise, but she was in control, always in control when she had an end in mind.

Miss Yardley was a tall young woman, slender, and conservatively dressed in a muslin gown of coffee brown. Her chestnut hair was silky, long, and tightly bound in a knot at the top of her well-shaped head. Her eyes were soft brown, but they lacked any warmth. Her nose was aquiline; her lips were thin and at the moment pursed with little pleasure and some thought. She liked Arabella no better than Bell liked her. She did, however, observe the amenities and went forward with a polite greeting.

"Arabella. How very pleasant to see you looking so well. I had not hoped for so much in so little time."

Bell frowned, though the meaning of this had not yet hit. Rose put her hand on Bell's arm, for she did sense the implication hidden in the gentle words. It was not enough to forestall Bell, who was momentarily sidetracked by the comment. "What do you mean?" asked Bell, puzzled. "I have not been ill."

"No, no," answered Miss Yardley, "but all of us felt for you . . . after your colonel . . . er . . . left."

Arabella's eyes flashed. Here was a blow that deserved one in return, but now was not the time. She managed a sweet smile and said softly, "How kind." Quickly Bell turned to introduce Rose, adding hurriedly and without flavor, "We are here you know to offer you our congratulations on your engagement to James."

Miss Yardley was taken aback; however, she recovered and inquired in a seemingly calm voice, "Thank you, but how is it you know?" She shook her head over the problem. "We do not plan any announcement for another month and have told virtually no one. . . ."

"Never say, it is a secret!" Arabella sounded dismayed. Rose watched her friend with avid curiosity and amaze-

59

ment. She was seeing Bell in one of her finest performances and was thoroughly intrigued. What the deuce was behind it all?

"No, no . . . of course it is not a secret. . . ." Maria recovered herself. "It is just that I did not think the servants' grapevine worked that quickly."

"Oh, it does not. I had the news from James," said Arabella brightly. Through her dark eyes she watched Maria's reaction and was not displeased to find she had been right in what she believed.

Maria had been in the process of pouring tea and nearly spilled it. She once again recovered her poise, which was considerable. "From my James . . . you say? He has been to visit you, then?"

"Oh, I am lucky enough to see him when he comes to visit my brother," said Arabella kindly, for she had no wish to make Maria jealous.

"I see," said Maria thoughtfully. "He no doubt wanted Sir Robert's aid in seeking out a lodging for the season."

"No doubt," answered Arabella, "but there is no rush. James will be staying with us until he is established."

Maria stiffened. "I hardly think that is suitable."

"Oh, I know you are a stickler for the proprieties, Maria, but, you needn't worry this time. Violet is with us and lends us respectability."

"Violet Cullingham?" Maria considered this, her thoughts clicking away. This was a London hostess who could manage an entree for her to Almacks. To date, her own mother had been unable to obtain vouchers.

"Oh, yes. We are all one big happy family with Vi at the head of the table, for you must know Rose stays with us as well."

Maria smiled absently, thinking about what use could be made of this. She said after a slight pause, "You know, Arabella, Mother has had a difficult time obtaining vouchers for Almacks. . . ."

"Has she?" Arabella feigned surprise. The Yardleys were a wealthy lot, but their birth was low, and this would be enough to keep them from the famous club. "Well, I shall have Vi attend to it at once." Then, after a significant moment in which she allowed Maria to observe her frown, she asked, "But . . . my dear, aren't you in mourning? Wouldn't that preclude any visits to Almacks?"

"Well, yes . . . but only for the next month," said Maria hastily.

"Ah," said Arabella, getting up and turning to her friend, who also jumped to her feet. They had not touched their tea. "Then I will see to it immediately."

They had taken their leave, clamored into the coach, and turned to look at each other before Arabella released a series of giggles.

"You are a wretch!" said Rose. "What are you up to?"

"My darling Rosey, can you see my poor James married to that woman?"

"She is reserved . . . and possibly not a beauty, but I see nothing to elicit such behavior from you."

"Don't you? Then you shall before the month is over," pronounced Arabella.

"Bell, tell me what you mean to do. There is something cooking in that head of yours—I can tell."

"Can you? I don't see how, when you cannot see that . . . that woman is *not* in love with James."

"Oh, but she may be. Not all of us lay our emotions on the table as you do, you miserable girl!"

"I agree. Some of us are slightly, correctly, adorably reserved, as you are, my pet. There is a difference between being reserved and being cold as ice."

"Ah, and she, I take your meaning to be, is cold as ice?"

"Precisely."

"Well, then, perhaps James will melt the ice," said Rose thoughtfully.

"Never. They are worlds apart. Beneath his placid exterior, James is full of mischief, and Maria is bent on self-righteous, pious, staid living. They will never get along well together. Trust me." Then she eyed her friend, a certain impish grin transforming her features into those of a pixie. "Rose, you called him James."

"You are, of course, quite mad," said her friend blandly.

"So I am. Aren't we all in various degrees?" Arabella giggled. "But *I* know what I know."

"Do you? And what, pray, is that?"

"Oh, we shall see." Then, after a pause and a tug at her own amber curls, she continued. "For now we must go home and get ready for the masquerade tonight. I mean for James to accompany us, and he does not have a costume. We must see to it."

"Bell . . . how can we see to it? It is too late . . . and besides, I heard him tell you that he is dining with the Yardleys tonight."

"Ah, so he is, but he also told me that they dine early, which means he will be able to return home, change into his costume, and join us at the Rothman Masquerade."

Rose shook her head and said with affectionate amusement, "You are incorrigible."

"So I am, but just think how much fun we shall have all the rest of our days, for I can see you are beginning to understand me."

"Indeed . . . may the heavens protect me," laughed Rose.

Chapter Eleven

The Rothmans had quite outdone all others with their masquerade ball. Lady Rothman had been quite determined to display her ability and mark her place among the *haut ton* of London. This was due to the fact that she was only twenty years old, twenty years her husband's junior, and too often treated like a child.

She was a blondhaired, blue-eyed nonpareil with as much wit as beauty, and she was set on making her husband proud, for, in spite of the difference in their years, theirs was a love match. She watched London's best, some 350 in number, enjoy themselves in her ballroom, and she smiled. Indeed, the flowers were arranged superbly. The music was bright, lovely, welcoming. The champagne flowed freely, and a tasteful array of food was being served in her long dining room. Then, too, she had enlisted one or two of her notable friends to inspire still others so that nearly everyone had gotten into the spirit of the masquerade. This was an evening to be remembered. Lady Rothman looked across at her husband, and they exchanged smiles.

Arabella watched the Rothmans and glittered. It was so refreshing to see a happy couple now and then. Ah, well, evidently some people married for love! She looked across the room, and her heart actually skipped a beat. She knew him at once. There could be no mistake. Faith, but he was so handsome, even with the black mask across his eyes! It was the earl. It had to be. He was disguised as a pirate captain in bold gleaming black. He wore a black bandana over his dusky waves of silk and a tri-cornered black and gold hat rakishly angled. A black cape was loosely tied and hung over one shoulder, exposing his open-necked and billowing black satin shirt. A black cummerbund and black britches with high boots completed the outfit. Arabella stared thinking him a magnificent specimen. His height had been enough to catch her eye, but it was his style of movement (so peculiarly his own) that kept her glance riveted to him. A thrill swept her body as she studied him. Odd that he had chosen to disguise himself as a pirate captain, for she had donned the colorful clothing of a pirate's first mate. She wore striped britches, a white billowing shirt, red cummerbund, and a black vest. Her amber curls were tucked beneath a black bandana, and she wore one gold loop in her left ear. A black mask covered her eyes.

He looked at her from across the room. She was an imp of a woman with a bubbling magnetism that he would have known anywhere. They found each other almost at the same moment, but it was he who started toward her. He was bent on reaching her, and he did. They didn't say a word as he took her in his arms and easily guided her to the cadence of the waltz.

"Arabella . . ." he whispered as they moved in flowing unison to the lilting of the waltz.

"So I am, my lord."

"I did not expect to find you here," he said, for in truth men did not bring their mistresses of lower birth to such functions, but perhaps her gentleman friend thought the masquerade would allow him such license.

She laughed, and it was a musical sound. "Oh, I rather thought *you* might be here."

His brow went up beneath the mask. "Did you, my little

pirate?'' And with a low chuckle, ''Did you also know I would be captain of your ship?''

It was so lovely to tease him, to flirt with him. She would not believe his caressing tone, she would not pay heed to his words, and she would give him the same as she got.

''Oh, but yes . . . for we are kindred spirits, you and I . . . don't you think? Both of us pirates . . . bent on stealing . . . hearts . . . souls . . . whatever, whoever is unwise enough to sail within our reach.''

''And are you willing to take the chance?''

''What chance is that, my lord?''

''Of playing the game within my waters, for that is where you are now, my minx.''

''If I play the game, then you must tell me what are the stakes.''

''I don't deal in hearts and souls,'' he answered on a husky note.

''In what, then?'' she pursued, enjoying herself immensely behind her mask.

''I will give you my body . . . and take yours in return for as long as it may please.''

''You intrigue me. Can you give your body . . . and withhold your heart?'' she asked with some interest. ''I suppose so, for men are capable of such things.''

''And what of you? Have you given your heart?'' he scoffed.

She frowned. She was right. He thought her a cyprian. How very amusing. ''Alas, no, my heart is my own.''

''And your body?'' He eyed her and was surprised to find himself almost breathless as he waited for her reply.

''Would you believe me if I told you it has never yet been anyone else's?''

He pulled a face and looked at her hand. ''I'm afraid not, my little one, for you see, I know better.''

''Do you?'' She laughed then. ''Well, sir . . .'' The

dance had come to an end. "Perhaps you do . . . and perhaps you do not." She indicated a gentleman dressed in the garb of a highwayman and said, "A friend of mine is waiting for me there . . . and I dare not disappoint him."

The earl frowned as he studied the highwayman. This was neither of the two young men he had seen her with in Dorchester. This was someone new.

"Arabella," he said, and held her wrist, "I want to talk to you."

"Do you, my buck?" She was saucy now. "Perhaps later . . . but for now my hand is claimed for the next waltz." She moved away and went to James, whispering, "James, James, dance with me at once, for there is someone I want to avoid."

"Yes, of course," he said, taking her up in a comfortable hold. "But have you seen Rose? I was talking to Robby and she was at my elbow . . . and then suddenly she was gone. . . ." He saw her on the dance floor with some young lad and said lightly, "Oh, there she is. . . ."

"Yes, she *is* pretty in that flower girl costume, isn't she?" said Arabella glibly, eyeing him sideways as he responded.

"Beautiful, but it is more than just her look. There is something in her eyes that shines . . . and she is so easy to talk to. She understands immediately what one means. . . . Well, I expect you know that."

"Yes, I do, and how very clever of you to discover it after only two days' acquaintance with her," said Arabella, a sure glitter in her dark eyes.

He didn't catch the look which was just as well, for she didn't wish him to know what she was thinking. It was too soon for anyone to know what she was planning. She had a great many moves in store for her players if they were all to end up happily ever after, though she wasn't quite sure how she was going to manage it.

The waltz was over, and there he was again, her pirate

lord, stealing her attention. He grinned down at her and took up her hand. "And now, minx, you are promised to me."

"My lord . . ." she started to object.

He turned and peered deeply into her eyes, saying softly, "Don't fuss, little one. You have nothing to fear from me."

"You are wrong, my lord," she returned almost breathlessly. "I have a great deal at stake." He had by this time maneuvered her into the garden. There were a great number of people milling about the stone patio, so she did not at first feel herself to be in any grave danger. She underestimated her man.

He watched everything around them as he spoke, and just as all gazes were elsewhere, he took her to the side of the building. She found herself with a thorny rose bush on one side, an oddly shaped and prickly pine on the other and the earl hovering above her. She was about to speak, but there wasn't the opportunity, for already his head was bent and his mouth on hers.

She hadn't meant to allow him this. She hadn't meant to allow her arms to wind up around his neck, and she certainly did not mean to respond to his kiss with such . . . force. This had to stop, and she told him so.

"Stop," she said as firmly as she could. "You . . . just have to stop. . . ."

"Why?" He was now nibbling on her ear, her neck, back to her ear.

She tried to think of a good reason to give him. "Because," she answered, for lack of anything else to say.

"Ah. Of course . . ." he whispered, and moved back from her. "As you wish."

She was amazed, startled, and just a little disappointed. After all, he could have fought a little bit harder for her kisses. She pulled herself together and started to walk off.

He held her to him once more. "Arabella . . . you were made for me, and I will have you in the end."

"Will you?" she retorted, her chin up but her body trembling all the same. "We shall see."

He followed her back into the ballroom, where she moved toward her brother. He saw her take up Robby's hands and frowned. How could she go from his kisses into that puppy's arms? It was outrageous, and it filled him with a sure but low-keyed jealously. She turned and saw him across the room, and for a moment her heart beat wavered on the pounding of hysteria. Such a look as he gave her! What, just what was happening?

Some moments later she watched as he took leave of his hostess and departed with friends. She felt a ridiculous sense of loss, and for her the rest of the evening had lost its sparkle. Later that night she lay quietly in her bed and thought of the earl. This was no good. The game now had to come to an end. She was becoming too attracted to him, and that was not supposed to happen. There were enough young men already paying her court. There was young William, in fact, who was tall and handsome and full of charm. Yes, she would concentrate on the hazel-eyed William and put thoughts of the earl and his deep blue eyes aside. She had to keep her distance. . . .

Chapter Twelve

The next three days had Arabella in a frenzy of restlessness. She put the reason for such a state at her aunt's door. Violet had decided that the week before the ball, she would curtail the social activities of her charges. What is rare, she told the girls, is most sought after!

Arabella paced before a moderate fire crackling sweetly in its grate in their library. Violet was with the housekeeper, finalizing last-minute orders for the ball. The young men of the household were out for the day, and only Rose sat contentedly glancing through the pages of a fashion plate. Bell pulled a face and demanded her attention.

"Rose!"

"Hmmm," answered Rose without looking up. Better to allow Arabella free rein for the moment. She would quiet after a bit.

"I can't bear it, Rose. Even sitting to dinner with that pompous Felix Standish would be better than another dull evening at home!"

"Now, that is doing it too brown, my girl." Rose grimaced. "Felix Standish indeed!" Rose eyed Arabella thoughtfully. "Can't think why Mr. Standish singled you out . . . but there never is any accounting for taste."

"Miserable girl, and you call yourself my friend," re-

69

torted Arabella playfully, for she could generally be teased into spirits.

"No," answered Rose sweetly, "*you* call me your friend!"

Rose got her curls tugged viciously and then found herself bear-hugged. "Well, at least there is you," laughed Arabella.

"Oh, that is a compliment," bantered Rose, for she knew her friend was blue-deviled at heart and thought to bring her out of it.

Arabella smiled at her. "Well, that is one of my strong points—flattery. Perhaps I should use it on my pompous admirer when he calls."

"Ugh. Will *he* be calling, do you think?" returned Rose.

"Undoubtedly. Mr. Standish told me to expect him," sighed Bell.

"I see. So that is what has you so . . . bubbling?" baited Rose gently.

Arabella eyed her and said nothing to this. She proceeded instead to do a tour of the room.

"You miss him." It was a flat statement with no opinion voiced in word or tone. Rose waited for Bell to look at her, and when she didn't, she pressed further, "You miss your earl of Magdalen?"

Arabella stopped and regarded her friend from drawn brows. "Perhaps . . . but I think if I were . . . playing about town a little . . . I would not."

"Oh?" Rose glanced up briefly at this but still gave away nothing. She was lounging in a chair with her back against one arm of the chair and her legs dangling over the other. She swung one leg and smiled just a bit tauntingly. "Good, then tonight you shan't miss him at all."

Arabella's pacing came to an abrupt stop, and she went to drop—heedless of her white muslin gown—to the Oriental carpet beside her friend's chair. "Explain!"

"James says he shall take us to the theater tonight to see

Kean. Says Aunt Violet has given her permission and that Robby and Freddy will make up our party as well.''

Arabella clapped her hands. ''Why, you wretch! This is famous good news. You . . . why, Rosey, you knew all along and kept it from me.'' She ended with a laughing accusation.

''Didn't keep it from you. Just told you, didn't I?'' returned Rose blandly, but the smile was in her eyes. ''Now, Bell, if you meet the Earl tonight . . . you must tell him who you are. This absurd game you have been playing with him must end.''

''I suppose . . . but it has been such fun, Rose,'' Arabella sighed.

''Yes, but you are playing with fire, and my girl, you don't have the knack yet. You will surely get burned.''

''*Not* if I keep far enough away from the flames . . .'' teased Bell.

''How can you when they are of your making, you abominable girl!'' retorted Rose in some measure of amusement.

The Theatre Royal, Drury Lane, reverberated with the sparkle of London's fashionables, all bent on ogling one another as much as—if not more than— the performers who would presently be on stage. The magnificence of the theater had only recently been restored after its devastating fire in 1809. This night, Edmund Kean was to star in a production of *Hamlet* and the ''pit,'' which catered to the middle class, was near to overflowing.

It was a ''first'' for both Rose and Arabella, and they sat in their box quite awestruck by the glamour of it all. Vi had already fluttered off to a nearby box to chat with friends, leaving Robby, Freddy, and James in attendance. They chose to go off to blow a cloud in the corridor with some cronies, so the burden of conversation with Miss Maria Yardley was left to the girls.

71

This, thought Arabella with irritation and she voiced into her friend's ear at the first opportunity, was beyond everything annoying! That James should extend the invitation to his fiancée, she could understand, but that Maria, who was supposed to be in mourning, should accept was a piece of unforeseen ill fortune!

Rose did not reply to Bell's lamentations, however; she too felt very much like boxing James's ears. After all, if he wanted to marry the prosy chit, that was his right, but it was not his right to foist her upon them! She calmed herself, chatted politely to the haughty Maria, and told herself she was overreacting.

Maria lightly touched Rose's arm. "Do you see that young woman in the box across from us?" she asked in a confiding manner.

Rose sensed danger and was wary in her reply as she returned to Maria, "Y-yes?"

"That is *the* Miss Diana," returned Maria portentiously.

"Ah," said Rose, and then, though she told herself she shouldn't, she asked, "Who is *the* Miss Diana?"

"Why, she is ward to Mr. Grenville and will one day inherit the largest fortune in all of England."

Rose eyed the young woman in the box across from theirs and then found Arabella's laughing dark eyes, for obviously Maria had more to say on the subject. Rose felt leery about it and gave the girl no more encouragement. However, Arabella's curiosity was too much for her, and it was Bell who urged her on. "She is a pretty girl."

That was all that Maria needed. "Hmmm. Your brother Robby thinks so." There was a smirk on her face, in her eyes.

"Does he?" returned Arabella. "He has excellent taste in women, but how you should be aware of it is more than I can fathom."

Danger! Danger! Danger! Rose knew this was the time

to change the subject. "Ah . . . I think the curtain will go up presently."

"How do I know?" returned Maria, who cordially disliked both Sir Robert and Arabella. "Why, it is all over town how Robert made a cake of himself the other night."

Rose's white-gloved hand quickly checked Bell's hot temper. She touched her soothingly and smiled at Maria and said, "Gossip, Maria, is so unbecoming . . . and you can ill afford it."

Violet entered the box in a flurry, to find Maria in a huff, Arabella in a temper, and Rose raising her brows. She attempted amiable conversation, but this was a difficult thing, as only Rose would take part. The reentry of the young men and the curtain going up were circumstances poor Violet was thankful for.

The earl pushed away his dinner and sighed. He was feeling restless and dissatisfied. He signed for one of his servants to remove his plate and sat back in his chair. His richly furnished dining room faded as he saw a pair of dark bright eyes glitter in a face filled with mischief. Amber curls bounced in sunlight, and a musical giggle nearly made him smile. Arabella. Everything about her had totally caught his attention, his imagination, his desires. She was the very heart of his turbulent moods these days, and there was no longer any denying it.

Damn! This was absurd. He had taught himself quite a long time ago not to allow any individual, especially a female, to dally with his emotions. This, however, he told himself over and over again, was quite different. Wasn't it? Yes, damnation, it was! He was used to getting his own way. He prided himself on the fact that when he wanted something badly enough, sooner or later he got it. Well, he wanted this chit, and he was going to have her. Somehow . . . and soon, for he had been waiting it out too long now. He was going to get her into his bed. The notion fairly stirred him, but these urgings were soon interrupted by the sound of his friends making their way toward the dining room.

The door was already opened, and he looked to find two lively men, arm in arm and grinning broadly. "Told you he was back in town," said the taller of these two.

The earl's butler squeezed past these two men and bowed an apology. "I told them you were having your dinner . . . but . . ."

The earl smiled and dismissed his man amicably, "It's all right, Foster. You never stood a chance." He rose and went forward, but not to greet the two gentlemen swaying in some glee within the dining room's wide doorway. Instead he put out his hand to another man who had been standing just a little apart, disdainfully regarding these two from a quizzing glass.

"Beau . . . to what do I owe this pleasant surprise, and why in heaven's name did you bring these two fools with you?" The harshness of these words was coated with affectionate amusement, and hence the two fools continued to smile . . . foolishly.

Beau Brummell put up his eyes heavenward and sighed. "Forgive me, my dear Shaun, but I brought them nowhere. I announced my intention of collecting you for the last act of *Hamlet*, and there was nothing for it but they must tag along." He eyed them from head to toe. "However, they will make good company for you, Shaun, for I can see that you are dressed no better than they."

Shaun threw back his head and laughed. Beau Brummell was London's leading dandy, but gone were the colorful silks and satins of another year. He had brought into fashion the exquisite cut to a man's coat, he had brought into style the need for bathing instead of heavy perfumes, and he had quite caught London's *beau monde* by storm with his excellent taste.

"I wasn't expecting *you*, or I should have taken more care with my cravat. . . ."

"And the choice of your coat, no doubt . . ." drawled the Beau.

Shaun's hand came down on his friend's shoulder. "Ah, don't I do you credit, my Beau? Forgive me, I shall take my punishment and stay home!" His blue eyes were glittering playfully.

"No, you shall take your punishment and accompany us." The Beau smiled.

"Ha!" cried Alvanley. "Got you, ol' fellow. But let's have another brandy before we trot off."

"Later, lobcock . . . no time . . ." answered the friend, leaning on him for support. "No time . . . end of first act soon. . . ."

"Right, then," returned Beau, turning away, "shall we?" He started off, never looking to see if anyone followed.

The earl was fond of Beau Brummell. They had been friends for nearly ten years. However, Shaun was his own man and rarely allowed the Beau or anyone else to dictate his moves. Yet tonight he fancied he rather needed a night out with his friends. Right. He collected his top hat, cane, gloves, and caped cloak on his way out and fell in step beside the Beau. At their backs, Lord Alvanley and John Swindon sang a wild chorus or two, and so they passed the distance to the Drury Theatre.

Chapter Thirteen

Intermission arrived just in time, for in spite of Kean's wondrous performance and Arabella's love of Shakespeare, her mind kept wandering to Maria's remark and to the fact that Robby was indeed gazing raptly not at the stage but at the girl in the box directly opposite theirs.

Vi announced her intention of visiting the box adjacent to theirs to chat with the Jersey while the young people went off for refreshment. Arabella was in a frenzy to get her brother off alone, and when they were in the hallway she did manage to ask him, "Robby . . . what is this I hear?"

He opened his eyes wide. "About what?"

"About you, dunce! And don't try to fob me off, for it won't work. Are you mad for some wretched girl who won't have you?" Arabella was always to the point, and more direct with her brother than anyone else.

His face took on a grim expression, and he answered her coldly, "I thought my sister would not listen to gossip, let alone repeat it."

"Then it is not true?" she questioned still further, for she knew him too well.

He meant to put up a front but suddenly broke down. "Aw . . . Bell, she is everything that is wonderful . . . and thinks me the lowest beast on earth!"

Arabella was rarely left speechless, but this was certainly a leveler. She could think of no response. Here was her older brother, whom for too long she had thought the sun, the moon, and the earth. How could anyone think him a beast? It was impossible, and therefore the girl in question was certainly not worth her salt! On this last notion her voice returned, "Upon my soul, Robby, the girl must be dashed queer in her attic!"

"You are not to say that of her. She is an angel. . . . Bell, mine was the fault. . . ." His ungloved hand ran nervously through his rust-colored waves of hair as he spoke and then faltered.

They were interrupted at that moment by the others in their group, and Arabella could have stamped her dainty little foot with vexation. What was all this? When had it occurred? Who was this girl? Why did she think her wondrous brother a beast?

Maria Yardley was drawling some nonsense or other and Arabella eyed her with fulmination for a moment. James was looking bored to tears with her, and Freddy was looking about him for some diversion, for it was plain he could not abide Miss Yardley's mode of conversation. It was unthinkable that James should be saddled with such a wife. She was a self-righteous prig with not an ounce of humor in her soul. They were totally unsuited for each other. She looked for Rose and noticed her moving off with Lady Sefton toward the main hallway. Out of the corner of her eye she could see that James too was watching Rose's departure. Bell smiled. Yes, Rosey was looking excellent in the soft yellow silk she had chosen to wear. The yellow feather curling around one ear was beautifully concordant with the tawny curls that framed her lovely face. There must be a way to get these two together, but for now, she was bound and determined to escape Maria's prattle!

"I think I shall go and see what Lady Sefton and Rose are about. . . ." She did not wait for anyone's objection

77

to be put forth but picked up the skirts of her pretty pale green muslin and started off. However, when she reached the long corridor, she could find no trace of Rose or the Lady Sefton. She stood for a moment when a light at the far end of the corridor caught her interest, and she moved in its direction. She soon discovered that it was the light to the backstage stairs. Biting her lower lip with mischievous intent, she started down the steps to explore. She hadn't gotten very far when the sound of a man's laughter froze her in place. It was a familiar sound, and it was close. She couldn't move. A moment later she was gazing down into brilliant blue eyes.

The earl and his friends had visited Kean in his dressing room and payed their respects. They were now on their way up to their box; however, the earl discovered that the sight of Arabella left him immobilized. He recovered himself, and his mind went into action. He moved quickly and grabbed her wrist. Even as he did so he turned and waved his friends on.

"Go on, lads. Take the main staircase, and I will be with you in a few moments." He winked at Beau, who was in front of the other two.

Beau Brummell's understanding was, as always, quick. He turned and said with perfect sang-froid, "It would appear that you two are in the way, and it is left to me to remove you. . . ." To their surprised expressions, he added only, "Come along."

They made a languid retreat to the lower floor, where they would take the main staircase to their box seats. During this time, the earl was a man transformed. He felt the change in himself the moment he looked into her warm dark eyes so charged with excitement. Only seconds ago the Beau had remarked that the earl was unusually quiet. He had shrugged his shoulders and responded that he was weary from the long journey back into London. Now he was vibrant, filled with anticipation, alive, and all because she was here, saucily smiling at him.

"My lord, how very . . . nice to see you . . ." She waited only the space of a moment and then quickly made a decision to say more; " . . . after all this time."

"Ah, then I am flattered indeed, for you noticed my absence." He bent and dropped a kiss upon the pale green lace covering her fingers. "Did you miss me, my sweetings?"

He moved up so that no steps remained between them, and now she was looking up into his blue eyes. She wanted to give him flirt for flirt and was annoyed with herself when she discovered the truth somehow making its way to her lips. "Yes . . . I fancy that I did. . . ." She stopped herself and pulled a face. "I must go. This is no longer viable."

He threw back his head and laughed. He couldn't resist the impulse to touch her, and he did, bringing her chin up with his gloved hand. "What is not viable, my silly goose?" There was affection in his tone, in the manner in which he looked at her, in the softness of his lips as they brushed a gentle kiss upon her cherry-ripe mouth.

She felt a shock wave take hold of her body and crumble its reserve. She felt her knees melt and her ankles cave in. She held his arm for support—after all, what else could a tottering lady do? "You must not. . . . I shouldn't. . . . You simply do not understand."

"Oh, I understand, sweetheart. It is now only left for me to make you understand," he retorted with some show of arrogance.

She considered him for a moment and felt a softening sensation. He was obviously no better than the rogue colonel who had played with her young heart, but somehow he was different. It would appear that she had a penchant for rogues. She must get control of herself.

"I must go."

"Why? Worried about the proprieties?" He said this with almost a sneer, for it annoyed him that she wished to run away.

It was a mistake, that look. It shot a bolt of anger through her, and up went her chin. "Not in the least. I must go because it is my wish to be elsewhere."

"Ah, no doubt your lover hangs in the shadows . . . waiting?"

She frowned. After all, he thought her a "bit of muslin," a "fancy-piece," because she had not corrected this notion. He thought her brother was her lover because she had allowed him to think it.

"My lord . . . you wrong me, and perhaps that is my fault. This is not the time—"

He interrupted, "Sweetheart, for too long now I have found that when we meet, anywhere we meet, it is the time, though perhaps we have not yet hit upon the right place." So saying, he took her up in his arms.

She put a gloved hand to his chest. "No, oh no, my lord . . . pray, you must not. . . ."

Still, he did. His mouth on hers was at first a gentle testing until he had her lips parted and his tongue easily within. She saw shooting stars, and it was much the same for him. Forgotten were the surroundings, until a man's voice said her name in shocked accents, *"Arabella!"*

She jumped and looked up at her brother's fuming countenance and silently said, Disaster! To her brother she said sweetly, "Oh, hallo, darling . . . I should like you to meet the earl of Magdalen." Then to the earl; "This is Sir Robert Cullingham. I believe you are acquainted with his aunt, Lady Violet Cullingham." So saying, and while her brother was still unable to speak, she took the last step up to reach his side and take his arm. "Come then. . . .It must be time for the next act." To the earl she adroitly turned and said lightly, "It was very pleasant, seeing you again, my

80

lord. Perhaps we shall see each other in the near future."
With this last she hurriedly steered her brother away.

Robby had allowed this as he had no wish to create a
public scene with his sister in the center. However, as soon
as they were some distance off, he whispered in hissing
resonance, "Explain!"

"He thinks I am . . . a tart."

"What?" This was a shriek. He could not help it.

"Shhhh . . . where is everyone?" She looked around
and saw that only a lingering few remained in the hallway.

"In their boxes, where we must go if we are not to create
a stir, but you will tell me why the earl of Magdalen should
think such a thing of you!"

"So I shall, when you tell me why that pretty little girl
should think you a beast." To his sudden confusion, she
softened, patted his arm, and said, "There is always a
reason, a logical one, for these absurdities. We shall exchange them later, and in private, yes?"

He sighed and touched her cheek. "Yes, but tell me,
Bell. You aren't in for another heartache, are you?"

"If I am, I shall weather it as I did the last," she gur-
gled. "And no, I am in for the time of my life, for while
my colonel, dreadful boy, was a rogue . . . this one, this
rakehell earl, is quite a man and worth the effort." She put
a finger to his lips. "Hush, now . . . or we shall have
Maria's questions on our heads."

Swathed in her soft yellow silk wrapper, her matching
silk slippers covering her feet, and a matching and rather
fetching nightcap set naughtily upon her amber curls, Arabella made her way down and across the long hall to her
brother's bedchamber. There she knocked soundly, received a welcome, and peeped in.

"It's me . . ." she offered superfluously, and smiled as
she entered the dimly lit room.

Her brother stood in his dark maroon brocade dressing

gown. He was frowning as he pulled at his full lower lip and gazed down into the fire burning in his marble-framed grate. He managed a smile for her and said, "And it's about time, madcap."

She ran to him then as she had so often during the years. He had been brother, father, friend, for so long that it was a most natural thing, and he opened his arms wide to receive her. "We have a bit of a fix on our hands, eh, girl? Both of us unlucky in love . . ."

She slapped his shoulder and stood away from him. "What is this? A Cullingham giving up? Never. Now, you first. Tell me about this wretched girl who thinks you are a beast. What did you do to her, and when did you do it? All this while I thought you and Freddy madly in love with our Rose."

He had the good grace to blush and throw up his hand in exasperation. "I know, I know. But Bell, when I saw *her*, why, it was as though I had been struck on the head. I was stunned by the sight of her. Oh, Bell, I have made a terrible work of it."

"How, why? Oh, do stop pacing, Robby, and sit here by the fire and explain," she coaxed urgently, and dropped onto the hearth rug.

He complied and then took a long breath of air. "It is a long story . . ." he offered.

"Am I running anywhere?" she answered saucily.

"Right, well, Bell . . . you see . . ." He sighed again. "It was all for a lark, and we were fuzzed, badly foxed, you know, and there it was."

"There what was?" she said, her dark eyes wide.

"The performing bear."

"Well, of course. A performing bear!" she retorted abruptly, cutting off a giggle, for she could see this was serious business. "So there it was, this performing bear, and you being in your cups?" she urged.

"Aye, so there we were. . . ."

"Who was 'we'?" Arabella liked to have all her facts.

"Freddy, this chap Harry from school whom we had just happened to meet . . . and I. Well, there we were on the Thames for that haymarket fair, you know—"

"You *are* a beast!" said his devoted sister acidly. "*You* told me it wasn't the sort of place to go. You—"

"Never mind that now. Told you . . . not totally responsible when we went there . . . and *there* it was—this bear, you see."

"Right, right, the bear. So what about this bear?"

"I was trying to tell you, but if you will interrupt . . . I shan't be able to."

"I am dreadfully sorry, so do proceed," she returned on a meek note.

He eyed her doubtfully, but finding her quiet and complacent enough, he went on. "Got it into my head I would bring him home for you . . . and Rose."

"Why, Robby . . . how nice. I think I have always wanted a performing bear." With this she did go off into a bout of indecent mirth.

He waited patiently for this to subside and said in frosty tones, "Shall I continue?"

"Yes, please." She was wiping her eyes.

"Well . . . the thing was, we weren't quite sure how we would transport it once we got it to the main thoroughfare."

"Ah, things are becoming clearer. . . ." Still another giggle escaped her, but she managed some control, seeing that it would be the prudent thing.

"So there we were in the street . . . the three of us rather badly dipped, somewhat jolly, and determined to bring this bear to Grovesnor Square and you." He shook his head and smiled. "*Certes*, if you could have but seen us, Bell . . ."

"I am seeing you . . . vividly," she squeaked, and lost

control, doubling over in a most unladylike manner and laughing near to split.

He broke down momentarily as well as he recalled the scene of his friends attempting to flag down a hackney, and then he remembered what then occurred and sighed sadly. Bell saw this at once and managed to urge him gently, "What happened, Rob?"

"A coach slowed to a halt . . . *her coach*." He added this last most tragically.

"And you asked her to squeeze in with the bear?" Arabella felt the giggles returning.

He depressed this with a severe frown. "No, I came to my senses the moment I saw her, but it was too late . . . for what must she do but jump out of her coach with her duenna at her heels chirping at her and us."

"But why?" Arabella asked in some surprise.

"I don't know exactly. It seemed the bear took a swipe at Freddy just before she got out, which she didn't see, but she did see Freddy take off his hat and beat the 'poor furry thing,' as she called it."

"Freddy wouldn't!" objected Arabella.

"Ah, that is what I tried to tell her. Oh, Bell, if you could have but seen her." This was said with overall admiration very near to worship and almost made Arabella sick. To hear her brother swoon over a woman was a new experience.

"She would have it that we were fools on a lark and said that while we had every right to debase ourselves, we had no right to drag along a poor helpless creature."

"She has a point," offered Arabella reasonably.

"I told you already that she thinks me a beast. Would she do so if I hadn't given her reason?" he asked sadly.

"Oh, do shut up and proceed. Then what happened?" Bell returned impatiently.

He ignored this contrary command but did go on with

his tale. "Right. Well, the thing is I sobered up as soon as I clapped eyes on her. I don't know how that is, but it is."

"Odd, that," interrupted Bell with some interest. "Perhaps you only thought you did. . . ."

"No, no, I tell you. Everything became clear all at once. Well, at any rate, I said we would return the bear to his owners. I tried to apologize to her for offending her principles."

"Well, you did all any offended woman could want." Bell smiled. "So I don't understand why . . ."

"She was just softening. I thought I had just managed to get a smile from her when the cursed bear took it into his head to go after Freddy again."

"Oh, no . . ." groaned Bell.

"What could I do? Freddy was raving like a lunatic that the bear meant to eat him, and for a moment there, Bell—well, I did wonder—but I couldn't let the bear have at Freddy, now could I? And there was Harry, incapable of standing, let alone fighting off a bear."

"What did you do?"

"Well, there isn't much you can do with a bear, you know—big sort of creatures with rather fancy teeth—but its owner said it was tame and should it get testy, we should slap its face and it would back down."

"So you slapped its face," she stuck in with a shake of her head. "Hence, you are a beast."

"There you have it."

"What happened then?"

"Miss Swindon—that is who she is, Miss Diana Swindon, for she told me who she was before she took the bear's lead and strode off with him."

"Never say she took the bear!"

"Aye, she did, with her duenna in tow, screeching enough to wake the dead."

"And you let her?" cried Arabella.

"Let her? Bell, I had no choice, but I did stay with her

until the errand was completed, and she read me a lecture the likes of which I shall never forget.''

"Oh, I do like her," said Arabella with a smile. "She is a girl after my own heart, and don't you worry, Robby, it will be fine."

"Will it? I rather doubt that. I went to pay her a morning call the next day to see if I could explain, but she wouldn't see me."

"Do you know that your name was taken in to her? Perhaps their butler turned you away without her knowledge. Perhaps she wasn't receiving."

"No, I had given her my name that night, and she sent a message with her butler expressly forbidding me entrance."

"Then you will send her flowers tomorrow morning with a letter explaining your position and asking if you might call on her," said Arabella.

"Do you think it will serve?"

"Better than doing nothing at all," returned his sister, getting up and moving over to drop a kiss on his cheek, "and if that doesn't work, there is yet another thing we might try."

"What?"

"Oh, no, I shan't tell you, for it might not be necessary. Good night, dearest Robby. Sleep tight."

"Yes . . . but Bell . . . ?"

"Hmmm?" She turned at the door.

"You still have not told me why you were kissing the earl of Magdalen."

"I was kissing him, my brother, because it seemed the thing to do at the time." With that she giggled and closed the door.

Chapter Fourteen

The morning was a clear, bright one, and a sunny ray singled out Rose's pretty form as she sat perusing the newspaper in the library. A cup of tea, half-finished, sat on the coffee table at her knees. She presented quite a lovely picture with her tawny curls framing her piquant profile.

James stepped into the library, his own cup of coffee in his hands, and he stopped abruptly to look at her. She did not hear him enter and continued to look over the paper. It occurred to him, this time more forcibly than it had the night before, that she was intriguingly attractive, perhaps more attractive than any other woman of his acquaintance.

Something—she did not know what—made her look around, and when she saw him she smiled and said, "James . . . we are both of us, I am afraid, up before the others and must wait for our breakfast."

"Rose . . ." He felt at a loss for words. He, who prided himself on his finesse with women, was at a loss for words. "I. . . . Your gown becomes you. . . ."

She looked down at the pale blue silk and then back at him and, for no apparent reason, blushed. "Thank you." Then she looked at the paper and held it toward him as he made his way to the yellow damask sofa to seat himself beside her. "Would you like to look through this?"

"Perhaps later . . . but for now, I'd rather look at you."

He meant only a mild gallant flirtation, but somehow his voice resonated huskier than he intended, and his eyes caressed more than he meant them to.

She discovered that his voice, his words, made her feel almost shy and schoolgirlish. This was absurd. She looked at him squarely and returned, with just a show of sauciness, "Why?"

He threw back his head and laughed with genuine amusement, but then he did look at her, intently and very nearly tenderly, and said, "That is not how it is done, you know."

"Ah, what then? Should I have fluttered my lashes and blushed? Would that have served?"

"No, my pretty . . . not as well as what you did." With that he bent and dropped a kiss upon her lips. He had meant only to brush her mouth gently with his own, but somehow he found himself taking her into his arms; he found her responding, and then he was parting her lips, gently nibbling on her lower lip, sweetly kissing her in a way he was damned well sure he had never kissed a woman before.

Rose, she silently called on herself, Rose, think about what you are doing. Hallo, Rose? She couldn't, wouldn't. At that moment she knew that she wanted this tall, handsome James Huxley. However, she was a rational, practical being, and even in the heat of the moment, she recalled a major problem and pulled out of his hold.

"Stop this . . . at once!"

He dropped his arms and did not at first look at her. She immediately became annoyed at his silence and said accusingly, "You, sir, are engaged to be married."

"So I am," he conceded sadly.

"Then how dare you!" It was more a statement than a question.

He looked at her full. "Because you invited it, my darling."

He had spoken the truth, but there is a time for everything, and this was not the moment for it. Rose fired up and her hazel eyes blazed at him. "Ah, so it is my fault!"

"It certainly is not mine. Tell me, love. Is it my fault that you are as lovely, as soft, as sensual . . . as irresistible as you are? When I look at you, all others are forgotten."

These were excellent words, more so because he sounded sincere. She found herself softening toward him, and as she got to her feet she allowed gently, "We will forget this ever happened."

"Ah . . . perhaps you will, but not I."

The door opened once again, and Arabella came in, her yellow muslin flowing around her and her face alive with excitement.

"You will never guess . . . !" She drew up, narrowed her dark eyes, and surveyed the two people before her. "What have we here?"

Rose chose to ignore the question, leveling a warning glance at her friend. "What will we never guess?"

Arabella considered her. Something had just happened. She felt it, sensed it, knew it; however, she was wise enough to leave off questioning Rose until they were alone, so she returned to her merry tones and said, "Why, the Elgin Marbles!"

Rose looked at James for a possible explanation, and he laughed and said, "It is a midsummer moon with her . . . always has been."

Arabella laughed as well and shook her head. "No, no, you big dolt . . ." She moved to the newspaper and opened it to its mid-section to read. "Look. . . . Here it is, the Elgin Marbles will be on display . . . see?" She pointed and handed the thing over to James.

"Ah . . . yes, I have heard about them," he answered her, and dropped the paper onto the sofa.

"Well?" urged Arabella.

Rose was by this time busy reading about the Greek find

and did not bother answering Arabella's laconic question. It was left to James, who asked, "Well, what?"

"Well, do we mean to go?"

He looked at Rose, who seemed interested, because she quoted certain excerpts outloud. "Would you like to have a look at these limbless statues?"

"Yes, I rather think so . . . wouldn't you?" she returned with some animation.

"Yes, as a matter of fact. Come on, then, my pretties. . . . Get your bonnets and off we go!"

"No . . . not until we have breakfasted," returned Arabella, "I am famished, and besides . . . there is something perhaps we should do."

"Oh?" This from James, while Rose eyed her friend doubtfully.

"Hmmm . . . perhaps we should invite dear Maria to join us," suggested Arabella mischievously.

James's face fell ludicrously, but he conceded that it would be the thing to do. Rose waited only long enough for him to be out of the room before she turned and said in some surprise, "Now . . . that is not something I expected from *you*!"

"Oh? But why? They are engaged, you know."

Rose stiffened. "Yes, so they are, but until this moment I did not think you thought so."

"Oh, but you see, I do. The difference between us is that I don't mean for the situation to go on."

"Don't you? Yet you foster it by inviting her on our little expedition."

"With every good reason."

"With every good reason? What, for instance?"

"How did I know that the Elgin Marbles were available for viewing? I mean, Rose . . . do *I* look at statues?" She pulled a face.

Rose laughed in spite of her irritation. "How then, brat?"

"I had a morning caller who told me all about the blasted things!" Arabella grimaced as she recalled her session with this particular gentleman.

"You did? But . . . when? . . . who?"

"Ah . . . I had no chance for escape. I was coming down the main staircase just as Fritzy opened the front door, and there he was. I couldn't be away from home or indisposed as there I was, wasn't I?"

"Yes, but who . . . and so early . . . ?"

"Who do you think? Take a whimsical guess." Again Arabella pulled a face.

"Oh, my faith!"

"Exactly."

Rose giggled.

"It wasn't funny. . . ." Bell was tapping her lip thoughtfully. "However, it has served . . . I think."

"Yes, but you can't mean to flirt with Felix Standish!" Rose nearly shrieked, for there seemed to be some such notion in her friend's mind. She could see it, though she couldn't understand it.

"Flirt with Sir Felix? I do not intend to! Why, it would very likely shock him into an apoplexy, for if ever there was a pompous priggish plumpish twiddlepoop . . ."

"Oh, stop, stop, Bell, you terrible girl!" laughed Rose.

"Nonsense. He is all those things. . . ."

"He could surprise you. After all, he has already surprised me by showing a marked degree of interest in *you.*"

Bell was diverted a moment. "Yes, that is out of character for Felix, but you see, he means to . . . er . . . what did he say—ah, yes, curb my wayward disposition."

Rose's hazel eyes opened wide and her voice went up one octave. "No, no, he never dared say such a thing!"

"Indeed, he did, but there is hope for me, you see, because my lively spirits and humorous nature are due to my youth and no doubt will be considerably reduced by the time he takes me to wife!"

"You can't mean he said that too!" This time Rose was close to squealing.

"Yes, he did." Arabella very nearly grinned.

"Upon my soul!" And then after a pause, "Bell . . . how did you allow him to get away with it?"

"Oh, I thought I might find a use for my pompous Felix," said Bell vaguely.

"Use? What use?" demanded Rose, suddenly finding something to worry about.

"Never mind that. I told darling Felix that we would meet him after breakfast at the Elgin Marbles."

"Upon my soul!" breathed Rose again as she gazed at her alarming friend in horrified wonder.

Chapter Fifteen

Sir Felix Standish was his mother's only child. He was thirty, he was tall, and, though he had a tendency to stoutness, he had not yet taken on any great weight. His hair was a fair shade of light brown and fell in gleaming swoops across his wide forehead. His complexion was florid; his lips were too full, and his eyes were a vague shade of light gray. In addition to these interesting attributes was the fact that he had inherited his father's enormous estates and was considered one of the wealthiest bachelors in all of London.

To date he had proved impervious to his mama's offerings, for she was determined to supply him with a bride of her choice. Grandchildren. She would wag her finger at him and announce her need to have grandchildren. Hence, she was forever pushing lovely young women of rank (usually with fortunes of their own) in his way. These girls seemed all quite willing to play the game, for he was titled and wealthy enough to be of some consequence. Sir Felix, however, had not fallen for their lures.

As it happened, he chose to look in on one of Lady Sefton's private little dinner parties and discovered there a young woman he had never seen before. Arabella. She was not his mother's choice and certainly not the type his mother would have chosen, but, in spite of Arabella's frivolous behavior, he made up his mind to have her for his wife.

To this end, he actively, and in a most dignified manner, conducted his courtship. This had been going on for one week, and though he paid no mind to her gentle snubs, he did feel she could show a little more enthusiasm. That she might refuse his suit never entered his mind. In any case, he was excited (in his fashion) that she was willing to meet him at the Elgin Marbles and just a smidgen dashed to find that, in addition to her friend Rose, she had also brought with her half the world. He sighed. It was another of her habits he would have to curb, this propensity for always being surrounded by friends.

He moved toward her, ready to do the gallant and pleased to see her smiling at him, when her attention was taken by the young gentleman at her side, whom he recognized as Freddy Eastdean.

"Well . . . I'll tell you what . . ." Freddy was saying to Bell in unguarded accents. "It is as plain as pikestaff that this is a take-in!"

This caught the attention of Sir Felix and the company at large. Bell turned wide dark eyes to Freddy and inquired, "A take in? What do you mean, Freddy?"

"Why, Bell . . . just look at these things," demanded Freddy indignantly. "Some of 'em are missing both arms. . . . And that one . . . damn, but it hasn't a head!"

This drew several chuckles, and Arabella left it to her brother to assuage Freddy's sense of injustice. However, she could see that this would not easily be done, for he seemed to feel that if he had to pay the entry fee, he was entitled to see Greek statues in their entirety.

She turned and disarmed Sir Felix with her smile, for he was at that moment thinking Freddy a boorish sort, beneath his notice. However Bell's charm distracted him a moment. "Ah . . . what a very fine cravat you have tied, Felix," she said sweetly, for indeed, its folds were most intricate.

He was momentarily diverted and took some moments to describe the labors involved in arranging the "waterfall," as it was known in fashionable circles. However, some chance remark of Freddy's caught his ear, and he frowned at him. "That one," he said witheringly, "is a fool."

Arabella felt her hands form into fists and her temper rush to her lips. She closed her mouth and restrained herself. "Oh, Freddy is a dear . . . not a scholar . . . but a lifelong friend to both my brother and me."

Rose had been standing thoughtfully to one side with her eyes fixed on nothing in particular, but she turned to Sir Felix and said, "Freddy may not have worded his sentiments to your liking, sir, but he did make a valid point." It was softly spoken, but there was the sound of intelligence behind the softness.

Sir Felix's haughty brow went up. "How is that?"

"Ah, well, you must know that these . . . marbles have cost a neat sum of thirty-five thousand pounds. We have people starving in London, yet we manage to lay our money down for something that is quite meaningless to the majority."

This was not a Tory point of view, and Sir Felix was a staunch Tory. He grew quite red in the face and blustered, "You can not put a price tag on art!"

Maria Yardley and James had joined the circle, and Maria interjected gently, "No, no, and this is more than art. . . ."

"Oh, I quite agree," proceeded Rose. "However, it is difficult to put a figure on the number of people that amount could have fed." She turned to Maria. "You see, I appreciate art as well, dear, but not above human life."

James found himself gazing at Rose sweetly as he said, "Anyone with sensibilities must feel as you do."

Arabella watched with glee, her dark eyes alight as Maria cast a reproachful expression toward her intended and said, "Now, James, I consider myself sensitive to the plight of others less fortunate, but I can not agree with Rose in this."

Sir Felix very nearly snorted, "Miss Yardley and I are one in this."

"Oh, for pity's sake," said Arabella. "Felix, art is art and will continue to be so, whether here or in Greece, where these artifacts originated. It is the cost of buying and bringing them to London that Rose has objected to, and rightly so."

Her brother laughed, for on this note Arabella abruptly departed, Rose in tow. He turned and offered, "I think we have had enough of marbles for one morning. Shall we go with my sister?"

"Yes, but . . . where is she going?" Sir Felix asked in some diverted confusion.

"I should think to have our grooms bring around the coaches," said Freddy. "We are promised at the Tavern on the Thames for a two o'clock luncheon, and it is nearly that now."

Later that day, Arabella nearly purred with satisfaction to find James and Rose laughing over the day's events in the cozy privacy of the town house library. She played chaperone for some fifteen minutes, interjecting comments whenever she thought the conversation needed some spice, and then quietly, with but a lame excuse, departed for the nether regions of the house.

It was in the kitchens that she found Violet in a flurry over the menu for the ball. Violet acknowledged her niece's presence with an exclamation: "Darling, I am so glad you are here!"

Arabella immediately grew wary. "Why?"

"Because you can help me decide about the lobster salad."

"You know better than I . . . ." started Arabella, spying

what she had come to the kitchens for and moving in its direction. She took up a chocolate confection with every intention of stuffing it whole into her mouth when it was rudely snatched away.

"No! The ball is in two days, and I don't want you growing out of your gown."

"But Vi . . . I am . . . hungry . . ." she pleaded, reaching for the chocolate.

"Go and busy yourself with something," returned Violet firmly.

Arabella eyed the sweetcake with a sigh and started off. Vi forestalled her with "But tell me before you go. . . . Lobster tarts with champagne?"

Arabella pulled a face. "Lobster tarts . . . ? Never."

"Never mind. I will handle this," returned her aunt with some annoyance, for she had every intention of serving this delicacy as hors d'oeuvres during their forthcoming gala evening.

Then, as though—and perhaps it was—an afterthought, Bell turned and asked lightly, "Oh, by the way, do you know Grenville's ward . . . ? I can't remember her name."

"Diana Swindon." Violet wrinkled her nose. "Quiet sort, rather pretty. She was brought out last season. Didn't take, though. . . . There was some fuss . . . can't remember what it was."

This intrigued Bell, and she returned to stand close to her aunt, noting that the servants in the kitchen weren't talking. She smiled to herself. They were a loyal staff, and anything that went on in the household had their entire interest. She said softly, "I can't imagine why a pretty heiress wouldn't take. Come now, Vi. . . . You must remember."

"Hmmm . . . odd, that. . . ." Violet puckered up her lips and put a finger to her nose. "That's it. . . . Poor girl, it wasn't that she didn't have proposals. She did, but the

97

one she accepted turned out to be a fortune hunter . . . and the banns were never posted.''

''What? Oh, the poor girl . . . but I don't understand. If his suit was accepted, how did they . . . ?''

''Yes, yes. That's right.'' Violet was speaking to herself as much as to Bell as she recalled the incident. ''Grenville never trusted the boy. He was French, you see . . . an emigré family, but he was worse than that. . . .Turned out he wasn't from an aristocratic family. Was a skirter. You see, on the fringe, made a living in the gaming hells. . . where he cheated. Oh, a perfectly dreadful boy, and Grenville paid him off to leave the child alone, which is what he wanted in the first place, you see, but the poor girl never forgave Grenville for it and has been carrying a chip on her shoulder ever since.'' Violet sighed. ''One can't really blame her. Men can be such unfeeling creatures.''

''Yes, but she should be happy he was found out before she married him,'' said Bell, frowning.

''Perhaps she thought some moments of happiness would have been worth the deception. I don't know. . . . But why do you ask?''

''I noticed her the other night when Maria was kind enough to point her out to me at the theater.''

''Maria? James's Maria? Never say she is a friend of Miss Swindon! I wouldn't have credited it.''

''No, no. She was being spiteful. Seemed to think that our Robby has a tendre in that direction.''

Violet opened her eyes wide. ''Never say so!''

''Would it be so terrible?'' Bell was watching her closely.

''Terrible? No . . . well, I don't know. I think the child . . . is somewhat bitter over her experience. I don't know that our gentle Robby will sweep her off her feet.''

''Don't you? But if the other had been a charmer . . . perhaps our Robby is just what she needs,'' said Bell thoughtfully. Then she asked, "Does she come to our ball?"

Violet thought about this. "Why, yes. I recall that when I received Lady Sefton's acceptance, there was a notation saying that she would be bringing Miss Swindon as Grenville is on a repairing lease in the country."

"Good," said Arabella, making for the door, "I will manage to make her acquaintance, then."

"Will you?" asked Violet with brows up.

"You may depend upon it." Arabella smiled and left her aunt to her menu.

Violet turned and found two serving girls watching her and, with a show of authority, set them back to work. To herself she frowned. She had no doubt that Arabella would indeed make the acquaintance of the Swindon girl. She was not willing to think past this point, for she was sure it would make her quake, so instead she returned her attention to the menu at hand.

Chapter Sixteen

Arabella looked in at the library and found Rose, Freddy, and James riotously enjoying a game of ducks and drakes. Quietly and without letting them know she had been there, she withdrew. Rose had promised to accompany her to the lending library, where she had a book waiting to be signed out. It wasn't for herself but for Robby, and she had promised to have it for him before dusk. Well, she wasn't going to bother Rose to leave now. . . .

What then? Her maid was at the dentist having a tooth extracted, so there was no company there. It was late into the afternoon, and she really shouldn't be seen about town without some sort of escort. She went to the study, but there found Robby closeted with his man of business. Again, quietly she withdrew. Oh, pooh! What was in it if she ran over to the library and fetched his book? She would be back before anyone even noticed.

Right, then. She went after her dark brown cloak, and, slipping it over her shoulders, she moved toward the front doors. There, Fritzy moved into position, and with a disapproving tone, he inquired, "Going out, Miss Arabella?"

She laughed and softened her words only with the mischievous peep of her dark eyes. "How *did* you guess?" She moved through the doorway. She looked back, though, for she knew he was concerned, and said lightly, "I shan't be gone long. I'm off for the library, so you needn't look so prim.''

"Yes, Miss Arabella," he returned, still disapproving.

She laughed and lightly skipped down the bluestone steps, pulling the hood of her cloak over her amber curls and crossing the quiet avenue. It was nearly five o'clock, she noticed as she hurried along and realized that she would not make it on foot. Perhaps she could hail a hackney.

The earl of Magdalen was just leaving his club. He turned the avenue, and whom should he see just across the street but Arabella! He had been thinking about her all through the night, all through the morning, and by damn, here she was! He started across the street when he saw her hail a hackney, and a sudden notion took hold of him. He rushed, and made it to the hack just as she was climbing within and giving her direction. Nimbly he climbed up onto the box with the driver and winked. As the wink accompanied a gold sovereign, it was well received.

"I should like to find a quiet avenue where I may . . . er . . . court the young lady within your carriage. You will take your direction after that . . . from me. Understood?''

"Ay . . . as long as ye promise that ye don't mean no 'arm to come to the little loidy," said the driver with a warning look.

"No harm . . . just a little sport." The earl grinned as the driver wielded his team and made for a part of London that would serve the purpose.

They had traveled no more than three minutes when Arabella frowned. She was acquainted with London enough to know that she did not recognize any of the streets they had taken. Was it possible he had misunderstood? She started to lean out her door to call to him when the door on her left opened and the earl swung within very much like a cavalier! It was a most wondrous entrance to such a romantic girl as Arabella, and after her initial shock she very

101

much wanted to applaud. She did in fact say, "My faith! However did you manage that, and how did you know I was in this cab?" There was a touch of admiration in her dark eyes and the tone of her voice.

He laughed, well pleased with her reaction, and for answer he took her into his arms. "Where you are concerned, my love, I make it my business to know everything."

She giggled and made no immediate attempt to pull out of his hold. "Ah, but you *don't* know *everything.*" She elongated the last word and peeped up at him.

His voice grew husky as he bent to brush her lips with his. "I know this. . . ." It was nearly a whisper as his mouth closed on hers, and the gentle kiss he had meant to give her grew into something wild and out of control.

She pulled away from him, breathless, startled, and now determined to put an end to their enjoyable game. It was going too far. "Please, my lord . . . you must stop. . . ." She had to keep her wits about her.

"Why must I stop?" There was a certain amusement underlining the cadence of his voice, and his blue eyes twinkled.

She looked at him full and was not afraid, though she told herself she should be. Here was a rogue, no doubt, abducting her for lecherous intentions, yet she was not really disturbed. And then a sudden fear did grip her, the fear that she had fallen in love with this rogue, for at that moment she could not even remember the other heartbreaker's name! "Please," she repeated, lowering her eyes, "I must get to the lending library before it closes. . . . There is a book there they are holding for my . . . for Robby. . . ."

He frowned. He knew by now that her protector was Sir Robert Cullingham, but it was a fact he did not like to think about. That such a puppy should own such a woman! "Tell me, love. Where does he keep you? Surely not in Grovesnor Square with his aunt Violet."

She blushed, but put up her chin. "You would be astounded to know, but please, you will cause me a great deal of trouble if you don't take me to the library. . . ." She looked imploringly up at him.

He hesitated. He wanted her, but she was definitely distressed, and that bothered him. "I find I cannot knowingly cause you one moment's agitation. Of course I will take you to your blasted library!" He knocked on the ceiling and called to the driver to change his direction. This worthy raised his eyes heavenward and commented on the vagaries of the gentry, but he did as he was told.

"And after the library . . . where shall I take you?" He had leaned away from her in order to better survey her expressions, which he found fascinating.

Her thoughts usually showed in her eyes. This was a fact about which she could do naught, about which she rarely even thought, until she saw that he was reading her mind all too easily. She blushed again, for she had been confused as to what to say to his last question. "You should just let me off at the library. . . . I can make my own way back. . . ."

"I am afraid I cannot in good conscience do that. It is my fault that it will be dark before you are done with your errand, and therefore I must escort you to safety. Besides, it will afford me that much more time with you."

What to do? Egad, what the deuce was she going to do? Fairly nabbled, her brother would say. Shut up, right and tight. Game was over, but no, she could still come around. "You may take me to Cullingham House . . . my lord."

"Blister it, girl! Never say he keeps you in the same house with the lady Violet!" He was shocked.

"I am afraid so." She wanted to giggle, but controlled herself.

"I don't believe you," he returned.

"Then take me there and watch me received by his staff," she answered. "I am held in much affection in that

103

house.'' She peeped up at him again. "Is that so hard to believe? I have never thought of myself as the best of people, but certainly not so repulsive as that. . . .'' She was again enjoying herself immensely, for his mouth was still just a trifle open, so she added, "Sir Robert, you see, does not refer to me . . . in the manner that you have adopted, my lord.''

"No? When he visits your bedroom . . . or you, his, does he not indeed?'' demanded the earl indignantly.

"Hmmm . . . no, even when I visit his bedroom—and I do that more than he visits mine, you see. . . .''

"Enough! There is the library. Go and get your book!'' For some reason the earl was wrathful, out of temper, and he himself would be hard put to understand why.

Arabella allowed him a tiny smile, but as she turned to jump out of the cab, her dark eyes were fairly blinding with pixie glee!

He took her gloved hand as she climbed back into the cab, her book under her arm, and he saw her settled before eyeing her thoughtfully and asking, "Your direction, my Arabella?''

She gave it demurely and smiled to see his eyebrow go up. Evidently he still did not totally believe her, and why should he? She was playing a May-game with him, after all. She loved the set of his firm mouth, the disbelief in his deep blue eyes, as the cab made its way to Grovesnor Square. She made no attempt at conversation, and apparently this suited his mood until he took up her chin and said, "Come, child, let us end this game, and tell me, do, where I should take you.''

"My lord, this may be a game, and perhaps it will end, sooner than you imagine, I suppose, but you are certainly taking me to my home.''

He frowned and studied her. "Tell me. . . . Does he mean to wed you in spite of his family? Is that why he has you installed in his home?''

Her eyebrow went up with her chin though she wanted to giggle. "Robby has not the least notion of marrying me. How could he?"

They had by this time reached her address, and she turned to give him her hand. He took instead her shoulders and said between gritted teeth, "Then damn the boy, for I mean you to be mine!" with which he kissed her hard and most forcefully.

She came away from that kiss breathlessly, but managed to whisper out, "But my lord, this is so sudden. . . ." With that she dropped a kiss upon his mouth and hurried, before he could take hold of her again, out of the cab.

He watched her as she took the steps in an almost schoolgirlish fashion. He watched as the butler opened the door, and he could see that the old fellow's smile was indeed quite affectionate as he ushered Arabella in. What was this? This was unheard of. Yes, Sir Robert of Cullingham may have been so lost in love that he might keep his mistress close by, but not with his aunt, especially Violet Cullingham, installed!

This was a chit that had him by the heart. A terrible admission, even silently to himself, but he had to concede that all thoughts were centered on this girl! A girl—she seemed no more than that; yet she was another man's mistress and behaved brazenly about the whole damn thing as well. She gave him her kisses. She took his kisses, yet off she went to the Cullingham lad! Absurd and wicked and . . . and how in hell was he going to have her? He had to have her!

Chapter Seventeen

Arabella returned, a twinkle lighting her dark eyes to find Maria Yardley in the library with James, Freddy, and Rose. The smile quickly left her face. However, she recovered, coming forward sweetly with a great welcome. "Maria . . . how nice. Do you join us for dinner? We are promised to ourselves for the evening, as all this racketing about has quite done us in."

"Why, thank you. I did tell Mama that I might stay over, if invited," Maria said in a honey voice.

"Did you?" returned Arabella, her voice matching that of Maria's. "How clever of you."

Rose's eye twitched, and she moved away from this exchange to speak to Freddy, who was looking over the evening newspaper.

"Ah, Freddy . . . our quiet evening . . . is no more," said Rose, touching his shoulder as she sat down beside him.

He looked at Maria and grimaced. "Prune face," he said beneath his breath. "A shame what she does to James."

"What do you mean?" Rose was frowning.

"Look at him," directed Freddy with his chin. "Looks fair blue-deviled, he does, and he didn't until she walked in here."

Maria glanced at Arabella, who was now slipping off her cloak and laying it negligently on a side chair.

"You were not to be found when I first arrived."

"Why, were you looking?" asked Bell, her bristles beginning to stand on end.

"Oh, I merely asked after you, and no one seemed to know where you were."

"Was anyone worried?" Arabella inquired with a frosty smile.

"The wonder is that no one was. Do you often vanish without advising the household?"

"As often as I can," said Arabella with a laugh.

"Arabella has her own way of doing things," put in James, gently attempting to steer his intended bride off this subject. He knew Arabella well enough to know that she was fast taking a pet.

"Ah . . . and no doubt . . . Violet was with you, for I haven't seen her since I have been here, and I understand that Rose was alone with James and Freddy playing at silly games—"

Arabella cut in sharply, "What is that supposed to mean?"

"Nothing. But my mama would not allow me so much unchaperoned time with a man."

"She wasn't with just a man. She was with two—and besides, we do as we please in Cullingham House!" Arabella had most definitely taken a pet.

They were saved as Robby came stalking into the room at this point with a complaint about his agent when he noticed that Maria was with them. He frowned but managed to nod a quick hello to her, and then turned on his sister with, "Bell, did you manage to pick up that book for me?"

"Yes, Rob, it is on the table . . . there . . ." Arabella indicated as she took up a stale biscuit from the cold tea tray and bit into it.

Rose came over and, touching Arabella's arm, guided her to the sofa where they both sat. Rose whispered, "You were gone dreadfully long. Why didn't you take me with you?"

"Never mind that now, Rose. I have had the most marvelous adventure."

"Drat you!" returned Rose. "You always go off and have these 'marvelous' adventures!"

"Yes, but my earl very nearly abducted me . . . jumped into my hired hack . . . just like a Don Juan. It was absurdly romantic. And then when I pleaded, he didn't abduct me but took me to the library, and then . . ."

She waited a moment for Maria to walk away again, for the girl had seen them whispering and sidled over in their direction. James saw that the two girls had their heads together and wisely guided Maria into conversation.

"And then . . . ?" urged Rose.

"And then he brought me here. . . ."

"He never!" ejaculated Rose, and then looked around to see if anyone was listening. They weren't, and she sighed with relief. "Indeed. I insisted that this is where I reside with Robby, and so he called what he thought was my bluff."

"But Bell . . . then you still haven't told him who you are? He still thinks you are Robby's mistress? This is outrageous."

"Yes, he thinks that . . . and one can't blame him. All circumstances point in that direction."

"No, they do not. In fact, it is wondrous that he should think it, for all circumstances point elsewhere—the largest one being the fact that he now knows you reside with Violet Cullingham as well as Robby and Freddy!"

"Indeed, that, I think, has him greatly puzzled," giggled Bell, and then cautioned her friend to silence, for Maria was once again inching near. "All we need now is Felix to make this a perfect evening," she said under her breath.

Rose smiled indulgently and said, "You are incorrigible."

"And you are . . ." Arabella began, "no, I don't think I will tell you what you are. It is too soon."

"What do you mean?" Rose asked in surprised accents.

"Never mind . . . Freddy . . . ?" Arabella called. "What do you say to cards after dinner?" Thus, she changed the subject, for a series of suggestions followed hers, just as she had known they would.

It was later in the evening that a certain dawning lit in the earl's bright blue eyes. All at once he knew what had been nagging at his mind. For too long he had found himself troubled over something he couldn't name. He was standing in his study, sipping at his afternoon tea, when it came to him.

In some agitation he went to his writing desk and started going through his letters. They were all neatly filed, and it took some minutes before he found what he was looking for. Finally, with a growl of satisfaction, he pulled out Sir Jasper's letter and read it through, stopping to read out loud that Rose Knoyles would be staying with Violet Cullingham in London.

"I don't believe it . . ." he said under his breath. "This is quite preposterous. How dare that puppy foist his lady-love onto Lady Vi . . . and young Rose?" The earl was nearly beside himself as he stood up and began pacing. He was in a rage of indignation, and it took some minutes of pacing before he was able to calm himself and understand why.

He prided himself upon his clear thinking. He thought himself a man who was able to take a problem apart and eventually come up with the best, the only, solution. Well, fine, he told himself now, do so!

Right. So here was young Sir Robert from the north. No doubt he had found himself this pretty, this vivacious Arabella. She was educated, she was refined, and therefore she must have had some breeding. Perhaps she was a nobleman's illegitimate daughter. Never mind. Whatever she was, she had given herself over to Sir Robert's protection. Right, we know that, he told himself. The question remains unanswered. Why is she installed in Sir Robert's home? Marriage? He had decided to marry the chit. A mésalliance, of course. He was but a young pup. . . . Could he be lost in love?

Surely Violet would not allow the lad to make a match of it with Arabella. Would she? Perhaps Violet did not know anything about Arabella. Perhaps the boy had presented Arabella under a misleading identity.

Well, hell and fire! Damn the boy for his impudence, for there was no way he was going to let young Robby have this girl! Bell was made for one man only, for him, and he was going to have her! Perhaps, just perhaps, he would put in a morning call to Rose at Cullingham Town House. Indeed, that was the ticket! He would visit and pay his respects to Rose and see just how little Arabella was held in the Cullingham household!

Chapter Eighteen

Arabella did not habitually use their town house's formal morning room to receive callers, as the room was not designed to her taste. It had a high ceiling ornately designed with gothic moldings. The room's color design was pale blue and deep gold; its rich furnishings and its undersized windows did not give her a feeling of relaxation. She felt she couldn't be comfortable in this fashionable setting. However, it was the perfect place to receive Sir Felix Standish, and that was exactly what she did.

The morning was in fact a dreary one, and she had a small fire burning in the grate. She sat on the blue satin love seat, directed him to the opposite blue upholstered wing chair, and began pouring coffee. "How nice of you to stop by, Felix. I only wish that my aunt were here to join us for coffee, but never mind. Rose will be with us momentarily."

Felix was torn between satisfaction that his sense of propriety would not be offended (for being alone with a young maid was not appropriate behavior in his estimation) and the desire to have private speech with the woman he intended to make his wife.

He looked at Arabella doubtfully and suggested, "You should not really be receiving me . . . unattended. . . ."

"No? Perhaps you are right." She started to get to her feet.

He touched the ivory of her lace sleeve and gestured for her to be reseated. "But of course, as you said, Rose will join us soon."

She felt a gurgle of mirth begin, but she restrained herself and commented instead on the weather. "It is too bad we are having such a miserable morning. I did so want to go for a ride."

"You enjoy your horses. I approve of that," said Felix thoughtfully. "No doubt you have a comfortable mare."

"Not a mare, and though I find him thoroughly comfortable, I am afraid some would not."

"Ah. Spirited, is he?" Felix clucked. "Did your brother choose him for you? I would see you more safely mounted."

"My brother would never dream of choosing my horses," she answered, simply attempting to put a halt to this line of conversation. He was fast getting on her nerves.

The morning room door opened and Rose was upon them, dressed in the palest blue morning gown trimmed with a darker shade of blue at the low scoop of the neckline. She did not at first see that Felix was in the room. "Your girl told me you were in here, Bell. . . . Whatever for?"

"Ah, Rose. Here is Felix come to pay us a morning call. Do sit with us and have a cup of coffee."

Sir Felix stood and moved to bend over Rose's hand, uttering a very formal greeting as he did so. Rose's hazel eyes found Bell's dark ones, and Arabella lost control. Something of a gurgle did then reach her lips. She bit it back, and it came out sounding as though she were choking. Felix turned and gallantly attempted to come to her aid. "Oh, my love," he was moved to exclaim in heartfelt accents, "what is it? Are you all right?"

This sent Arabella off into a spasm of whoops, which in

112

turn infected Rose. Rose felt a tickling laughter shake her control. Hence, Felix was astonished into remarking, "Really, I don't understand, Miss Knoyles. How can you laugh when your dear friend stands in need of our help?"

The door opened, and their butler saved Rose from replying by announcing in reverent tones, "The earl of Magdalen, Shaun Standon."

This had the very strange effect of bringing the room into total and almost immediate silence. Arabella went from choking into a state where she very much doubted her ability to breathe. Rose stepped forward as though to shield Arabella. Sir Felix was moved into a state of confusion in which jealousy reigned supreme. Here was Magdalen. Everyone in London put the earl as *the* Corinthian of the *beau monde*. Magdalen was wealthy; he was highly titled; he was handsome. What did he want here at Cullingham House? Arabella?

The earl had come asking to be taken to his uncle's ward, Miss Rose Knoyles. He had not mentioned Arabella, though he had hoped he might catch a glimpse of her during his visit. He discovered her moving to stand behind a large winged chair as Rose came a step forward. He smiled to himself, for Arabella was looking magnificent in her tightly fitting morning gown of ivory lace. Her amber curls were in windswept fashion around her pert countenance, and at the moment her dark eyes were open wide, so very wide. He felt an absurd urgency to move to her and take her into his arms.

Instead, he gave all his attention to Rose, bending over the hand she offered, "Ah Rose, my dearest girl," he said sweetly, coming up from her hand to look into her hazel eyes and thinking, no fool here, but proceeding to say, "forgive me for not having come to call sooner."

He was right. He had found no fool in Rose. She knew exactly why he was there and gave him measure for measure, saying easily, "Oh, that I can forgive." Her hazel eyes were alight. "Ask instead if I can forgive you for calling just now."

Arabella nearly went off into another choking spasm. Her Rose was a wonder, with her mild manner and her sharp tongue. She waited breathlessly to see how the earl would react.

He handled himself with style and charm and laughed. "Come, then, and introduce me to your friends."

If he thought to outwit Rose in this ploy, he had misjudged his opponent. She rarely gave anything away and had the situation in hand when she turned to look at Arabella, glibly saying, "Bell, you did mention that you and the earl are acquainted."

Arabella silently applauded her friend's social genius and managed in a voice that nearly squeaked, "Indeed . . ." she turned to Sir Felix and said, "But I fancy the earl and Felix here have never had the pleasure . . ."

It was left to Rose to complete the introductions and Felix to be his usual, talkative self. He did not disappoint the girls in this regard and kept the earl engaged in conversation for some ten minutes before the earl was able to extricate himself and move in on Rose. He could see that Rose and Arabella had their heads together, a circumstance that surprised him no little bit. Whatever was going on here? How could Sir Robert expose a gently bred girl to his mistress? Why did Violet stand for it? Marriage? Had the boy actually proposed marriage? Did they know about Arabella's relationship to Sir Robert?

"How do you enjoy London, Rose?" he managed to ask as he took up a position beside Rose on the blue satin love seat and watched Arabella move closer to Sir Felix.

Arabella never heard Rose's reply, for she was intent on giving all her attention to Felix, who seemed pleased enough with this and began reciting to Bell the latest *on-dit*. Bell laughed and fluttered and captured Felix's attention in her effort to ignore the earl.

The earl looked Arabella's way pointedly and said to Rose in a confidential vein, "A charming child, Arabella. Have you known each other very long?"

"Long enough," said Rose.

"For what?" he chuckled, keeping his temper in tow.

"For friendship," she answered, and looked at him full as she smiled. He would get nothing out of her, and she wanted him to know this.

"Ah, I see," he answered by way of advising her that he understood. However, he proceeded with an indication of his chin. "That dandelion seems bent on fixing his attention with her. Doesn't he realize she has been spoken for?"

"Has she been?" returned Rose, still smiling.

He put his finger to her chin. "Ah, Rose, I had not hitherto realized to what depths your understanding could reach. I have certainly been blind."

"Hmmm. You certainly have," answered Rose Knoyles, looking up at the mantel clock and standing as she said to both gentlemen, "I am very sorry, Felix . . . Shaun, but I am afraid that Arabella and I have been promised for the remainder of the morning." She held out her hand to Sir Felix, who was the first to jump to his feet. "Do forgive us . . . and thank you for calling."

Felix made his exit and turned at the doorway to make certain he was followed by the earl. He watched as Rose gave him her hand, and, satisfied, he went into the hall to collect his hat and cane.

The earl took his departure in a far more leisurely fashion, for he could not be so easily put off. Oh, he took up Rose's hand and bade her a fond adieu, and then he moved to take both of Arabella's hands and say softly, for her ears alone, "Do you think this round went to you, my love?"

"I didn't know we were in an arena, my lord," she answered, still feeling oddly breathless.

"For all the world to see, apparently," he answered,

and kissed the fingertips of both her hands, "until you cry uncle, and make no mistake, my sweetheart. You will."

"I have cried uncle once before and in so doing learned my lesson. He was dashing, handsome, and filled my ears with his compliments, and indeed, my lord, I cried uncle. I will not be so caught again."

He frowned. How young she was to have already been with so many men. This was outrageous. He couldn't believe it. This was impossible. He could see Rose moving toward the door, allowing them some privacy by giving them her back, and he said, "Arabella . . . I mean for you to be mine, and what I want I always get in the end. But do not think that I mean to hurt you. I wouldn't do that."

She laughed, and it was a hard, cold sound. "Oh, my lord, I know that, for you shan't get the chance!" She moved away from him and toward the protection of Rose.

He had no choice but to leave them. Stopping for the slightest moment at the door but without looking back, he continued his exit.

They fell against the closed door and then into each other's arms, neither knowing whether to cry or to laugh.

"You dreadful brat," snapped Rose, coming from a bout of laughter. "He left here now thinking still that you are Robby's light o' love!"

"Hmmm. An amazing feat of finesse. How could he! How could he find me here, in *your* company, under the chaperonage of Lady Violet, with Sir Felix paying me court, and still think me a 'kept woman'? Why, the arrogance of the man! How could he look at me, listen to me— for I sound educated, don't I, Rose? . . . Rose?"

"Well, at times you sound no more than a schoolgirl, but you never . . . No, you really never sound like a kept woman," answered Rose after a thoughtful pause.

"Just so!" returned Arabella tartly. "Well, he shall have his shock, for Violet tells me that he has accepted to attend our ball."

"Oh, faith. I don't think I want to handle this," groaned Rose.

"Don't be so fainthearted. This will prove to be the best of good sport!"

"Bell, you are going to leave my eye with a permanent twitch!" moaned Rose.

Chapter Nineteen

Grovesnor Square was alive with the hustle-bustle of vendors delivering their wares to the Cullingham House, for it was the day of the ball. No fewer than three hundred of London's *haute ton* had accepted their invitations, and Violet was quite pleased with the results of her efforts.

Sir Felix wielded his way through tradesmen's carts. He found the front doors held open wide, but workmen in shirt sleeves and leather breeches nearly ran him over as they moved to install an awning across the flagway. He watched in fascinated horror as another two men rolled a red carpet directly in his path, and he finally realized that he would have to jump out of the way. A friendly-sounding voice came to his aid from behind. "Hallo there, ol' boy. . . . Here to see Bell? Bad timing. She is off for a ride in the park with Rose."

"Impossible," retorted Felix in much surprise.

James strode past him and into the house, nodded at the butler, dropped his hat and walking stick onto the sideboard table, and proceeded toward the library with Felix fast on his heels.

"James . . ." Felix attempted to get Jimmy's attention. "I say, James . . . ?"

Easily, with athletic grace, James sidestepped two chambermaids overladen with bowls of potpourri. Felix nearly

118

ran them down, recovered, and picked up his step as James vanished into the library.

"James, really!" called Felix as he followed him into this chamber, and then abruptly came to a halt, for James had stopped just within the portal.

"Maria . . . ?" James said on a surprised note not altogether displaying pleasure. "Whatever brings you here at such an early hour?"

She smiled coyly and went toward him. "What sort of welcome is that, dearest?"

James blushed and remembered his manners. This young woman was going to be his wife. A flitting vision of Rose descended upon him, and he brushed it aside. "Of course you are welcome."

She smiled and gave him her hand to kiss. "I came because, as you know, I won't be able to attend this evening and thought perhaps I might lend Violet whatever assistance she requires."

"I see," said James sternly for this was forward, presumptuous behavior on her part and he could not approve.

"Felix," she said warmly, and moved to give this hearty young man her hand. "How very nice to see you. Are you here looking for Arabella?" She didn't wait for a reply but shook her head sadly and proceeded to advise him, "She and Rose went off riding. I cannot understand how they could leave Violet with all these preparations, but Arabella was always one for gadding about."

James found himself moved to expostulate, "No, really, Maria!"

There was no time for more, as Freddy and Robby appeared suddenly at the library's half-opened door. Perceiving the object of their quest they exclaimed in one voice, "There you are, James! We have been looking everywhere for you."

He went forward, concern in his blue eyes, for he could see they were agitated. "What is it? What is wrong?"

"Daffy!" said Freddy, who was obviously upset.

Daffy was Freddy's favorite hunter. He had brought him to London, for he meant to keep him exercised, but had been worried all along about the effects of London's traffic.

"Daffy?" questioned James. "What is wrong with Daffy?"

"Just now . . ." explained Robby, "we had a bit of a tangle with a vegetable cart. Seems to have done some damage to his hock."

"You'll know what to do," said Freddy, and then turned to Maria. "He's the best there is when it comes to legs."

"Yes of course, I'm coming. . . ."

"Oh, this is absurd!" objected Maria. "Can't Freddy's groom attend to the animal?"

"He *is* attending to him," said Robby quietly. "However, James has a knack with such things."

James bent politely to take Maria's hand. She gave it reluctantly, and with a pout that did not become her. He said apologetically, "I am sorry, my dear, but this is an emergency. I will no doubt see you before you leave."

"I should hope so," she said petulantly, and then turned to smile at Felix. "I suppose Felix and I can bear each other's company for the time being."

Freddy did a double take on that and said, as though struck by a sudden thought, "Wonderful notion, that!" He was taken in tow by Sir Robert and managed only a quick glance over his shoulder before his friends had him away. What he saw made his eyes glitter, for he could see Felix move toward Maria.

"Tell me, Miss Yardley. Do you waltz?" asked Felix as he took up a lady's chair across from where she sat on the sofa.

She opened her eyes wide. "Odd that you should ask that, for I was discussing the waltz with James just the other night." Then in a sad, confiding voice she informed him that she wouldn't be present at the ball, because she was still in mourning. He expressed his regrets, and encouraged, she proceeded, "Yes, but the month will soon be over, at which time I must come to a decision about the waltz."

"Only a month left, you say?" interjected Felix thoughtfully. "Then in all good conscience, I think you could attend the ball this evening if you refrain from taking part in the dancing."

Maria's eyes lit with this new fancy. "Do you think so?" Then quickly, as her mind sought a method of convincing her mama, she said "I wonder . . ."

"As to the waltz, I find I cannot approve of such a libertine dance. I know that it is sanctioned by the London hostesses; however, I will not have my future wife floating about in public in another man's arms."

"Indeed, you are quite right." Then in pure wickedness Maria could not refrain from adding, "Arabella and Rose both avidly approve of the waltz."

"Do they?" He shook his head. "I hold Arabella in the greatest esteem, but I cannot allow myself to be drawn into something on the whim of a woman, even Arabella. . . ."

Arabella, Rose, and Violet stopped at the threshold of the library. Violet sensed danger and immediately went forward with a lively greeting. Rose and Bell held their riding crops still; they exchanged a glance, and while it was certainly lively, it boded ill for Maria and Felix!

They entered in Violet's wake, and when greetings had been nodded and exchanged in polite fashion, Arabella gave Felix one of her frosty smiles and inquired, "What was that you were saying a moment ago . . . about the whim of a woman . . . and me?"

"Oh . . . that . . . ." said Felix, just a bit on the nervous side, for there was something in Arabella's eyes that snapped him to attention. "Miss Yardley and I were discussing the waltz. We don't approve of it, you see."

"Ah," put in Rose gently, "then neither of you must engage yourself to perform it."

Arabella checked a giggle and lost her anger. Felix nodded and added only that he hoped the woman he intended to make his wife felt the same way. Arabella put on a grave face and said, "Indeed, it is to be hoped that she feels the same way as you do, Felix."

Violet frowned over all this and said with some concern, "Well, that may be, but the waltz is sanctioned, and I for one wholeheartedly approve and . . ." She turned to Rose and Bell. "You, my darlings, I am persuaded, will be pleased to accept when asked."

"Of course, Vi," said Rose simply.

Maria decided to take charge of a conversations she was losing control of. "My lady . . . no doubt you have some last minute duties to perform. I should be delighted to take on whatever office you set me at."

"Nonsense. Everything that I cannot do is being done by the servants," said Violet with a laugh.

Rose saw immediately what Maria was up to and was quick to put down her pretensions. "Indeed, Maria, Vi chased us out of the house this morning so we shouldn't be in her way. . . ." She turned to Arabella and moved toward the door. "Bell, do let us go up and change now." There was a meaningful look in her eyes.

"Oh, by the by . . ." said Maria as a parting shot. "I think I shall see you tonight."

"Oh?" Arabella frowned.

"Yes, Felix was kind enough to point out to me that as it draws so close to the end of my mourning year, I might attend the ball and refrain from dancing."

"But how dull it will be for you. . . ." Arabella couldn't help herself. She had to discourage this girl from coming, but she could see it would do no good.

"No, how could it be with James there to bear me company?"

"Yes, but James is *not* in mourning!" Arabella snapped.

"A sticky point, that," put in Felix. "Should one's intended share such responsibilities?"

"It doesn't matter!" Arabella answered him testily. "They are not officially engaged!"

Rose stood during this exchange and said nothing. Violet chose the moment to intervene, for she could see that Arabella was about to say something outrageous. "It is such a pleasant surprise for us, Maria, that you have decided to join us this evening, and I am sure there will be enough going on here to keep you entertained." She turned to the girls. "Go on, you two. . . . This is a big night for both of you. Go on and bathe. For the remainder of the day, my dears, I shall keep you within doors!"

Chapter Twenty

Violet greeted her guests with both Freddy and Robby at her side on the receiving line. James mingled with the assembling company in the ballroom, which was beautifully decorated with flowers and lit candles. An orchestra played popular music while servants floated professionally about offering champagne, tidbits, and service.

Violet received Lord and Lady Sefton warmly and took a moment to exchange amiable conversation with Miss Swindon, who was looking quite pretty in her gown of pink and silver. The girl smiled sweetly at Violet and then froze as her gloved hand was taken up by Robby.

"Miss Swindon . . . I am so pleased . . ." he whispered, an amazing feat, as he had just caught his breath and nearly choked.

She was certainly a lady and recovered enough to be polite. Distant, but polite. "How do you do? Am I to understand that Miss Cullingham is your sister?"

"Indeed, and Miss Knoyles, a very dear friend of the family."

"There must be a very warm relationship for them to share such a night," she returned, for she had been brought up correctly and knew just how to behave on the social scene.

"Indeed. They are well suited," he was able to return,

and then: "I . . . I hope you may have received my flowers . . . and my note. . . ."

"Yes, sir, I did," was all the lady said as she passed on and found Freddy staring in some alarm at her. This so made her want to giggle that she nearly forgot her grievances against the two. However, she controlled the urge to forgive, merely nodded at Freddy, and proceeded to follow Lady Sefton into the ballroom.

"Egad!" breathed Freddy. "She is very proud, Robby. . . . You sure you want her?"

"Ay, I want her."

"Bring her down a peg, then, or you'll never have any peace," said Freddy, shaking his head. "She is too hard-hearted for my liking."

"You don't have to like her," snapped Robby.

"Damn, you're testy." Freddy pouted. "Think I'll go and have a look in at the ballroom. Leave you to do your duty with Vi alone."

"Well, then, go on," returned Robby in high dudgeon.

"That's what I'll do, then!" grumbled Freddy as he went off.

The earl of Magdalen entered and took a long moment to bend over Violet's hand. "You have done a wonderful job of it, Vi. This will be the talk of the season. The awning, the carpet, the flowers, are all perfection. It leaves only to see our sweet Rose descend."

Violet frowned, but then thought, of course, his interest is with his great-uncle's niece. "Yes, her gown is superb. She is wearing . . . no, I shan't tell you—you will see for yourself, for they should be coming down any minute. I sent Fritzy to fetch them, as nearly all our guests are here and waiting!"

"Fetch . . . *them?*" Somewhere in the back of the earl's mind a sudden light flashed, and he recalled the invitation listed two female names, Rose Knoyles and Arabella . . . Arabella Cullingham! It had never registered. He had never really seen . . . had never put it all together. How could it be? It was impossible, yet it explained so very much. . . .

Fritzy announced in resonant accents for those assembled and waiting in the ballroom whose doors were opened wide, ''Miss Arabella Cullingham and Miss Rose Knoyles.''

A hush followed this announcement as attention focused on the young women, for though a great many people had made their acquaintance during the preceding weeks, just as many had not. Then, too, the appearance of the girls was quite striking.

Rose had chosen a white, clinging gown embroidered throughout with silver fern leaves, and she had cropped her tawny hair in almost boyish style. She was quite stunning with the silver feather curling around one ear. Beside her, Arabella wore a clinging gown of organza that exactly matched her amber curls. It was delicately embroidered with bronze sequins, and a bronzed and glittery silk flower was attached just above one dainty ear. They made quite a picture as they descended the stairs.

Arabella saw the earl at once, saw his blue eyes glittering dangerously, and peeped saucily at him. How angry he was! What to do? Smile and brush it off. There was nothing else she could do. Ah, but she could see he wasn't going to allow her to do any such thing. Even now, with all the world watching, he was coming her way.

However, Sir Robert was already before him to take his sister on one side and Rose on the other into the ballroom. The earl had no choice but to allow this, for he would not willingly make a scene; but he did follow them into the ballroom, and it was not long before he claimed Arabella's hand and attempted private conversation.

''Do you think yourself any less a jade because you carry a name?'' he hissed, for he was angry.

She stiffened but managed a friendly smile. She allowed

126

him the right to be angry. "I told you no lies; you thought I was a jade and proceeded to behave like a rake."

"You encouraged me," he snapped.

"No, my lord," she said softly, "I did not invite you to jump through my hackney door or to force your kisses upon me everywhere we met."

"You did not discourage me!" He was frowning.

"How many times did I ask you to stop? How many times did I try to tell you that the game should end? I did not go in search of you and throw my arms around you whenever we met," she repeated.

"You invited my kisses . . . and by God, girl . . . you led me to think that Sir Robert was your lover!"

"I did not lead you to believe any such thing!" she answered, but still was not out of temper. She started off, but a waltz had struck up, and he took her arm and led her onto the floor.

"My lord . . . the first waltz should go to my brother . . ." she said, looking around for him.

"He is otherwise occupied, so it will go to me, for I am not finished!"

"Are you not?" She was speaking softly now, looking up into his blue eyes. "My lord . . . you thought me what you would . . . from our first meeting in Dorchester. Mine was not the fault. . . ."

"You go about at sporting events alone and unprotected and you say yours is not the fault?" He shook his head. "You allowed me to kiss you . . . in the theater . . . at Vauxhall Gardens. You kissed me in that hackney coach, if I recall. . . ."

"It was a good-bye kiss as I left you in the coach, for I knew you would soon know who I was."

"And . . . ?"

"And our little charade would be over," she said quietly.

"Arabella! Don't you understand? You may think it is over, but my girl, it is not!"

"Ah, do you mean to have me still? I understand that you are an honorable man and do not seduce virgins." There, it was out. Her cards on the table; the situation as it was. He raised his eyebrow, for he would not be trapped. The chit had somehow captured a part of him that made him feel as he had never felt before, but he would not be so easily caught. "And you, Arabella, do you mean to give your hand, your body, to a man you cannot love?"

"Pray . . . who is this man?" she returned, eyebrow up.

"Why, any other than me," he said arrogantly, yet somehow compellingly.

"Oh, no, my lord, you misread your woman. I mean to give hand, heart, and body to one man and one man alone, but I don't yet know who that may be."

The waltz had ended, and she found her brother ready to take her up for a cotillion. She dimpled at the earl and left him as she took Robby's hand. The situation nearly sent her into whoops, but she controlled herself and instead watched Rose exchanging light quips with James as they wielded steps together in the cadence of the dance.

The earl was not amused. He was in a temper, and the notion struck him that he should leave, but this was something he was not yet willing to do. There was something of a challenge in this situation, and he meant to see it through—even if it meant seducing a virgin!

Hell and damnation! He couldn't do that . . . not with a Cullingham. It would mean a wedding. What to do? An inner voice told him to leave and forget the chit. He moved toward the ballroom doors.

Arabella watched him as he strode toward the doors, and something inside of her cried. No, oh, no. If he went, he would take all the pleasure of the evening with him. She watched his broad shoulders in his black velvet as he reached the open double doors. Mentally she willed him to stay. He hesitated at the doors but did not look back. The next moment he was out of sight.

The cotillion came to an end and another was struck up. She found Felix at hand and forced herself to smile. She looked about, and seeing James in attendance on Maria, she could have stamped her foot in vexation. So far, very little was going along smoothly.

She answered Felix absently on some nonsense about the latest style of cravat that the Beau had introduced and was heartily glad when the dance had come to an end. She was again taken up onto the floor for another waltz by a young and attractive gentleman who managed to keep her interested for a time with amiable conversation. However, when this was over, she was feeling warm, tired, and nearly ready to cry.

She made her way toward the garden doors, stopping here and there to exchange remarks with friends and finally slipping outdoors. She saw him at once. He stood just outside the library door not more than twenty feet from her. She turned, ready to dart back into the ballroom. He stayed her with a soft word, her name: "Arabella."

She took a step toward him, but he was already upon her, taking her into his arms. She stopped him immediately, stopped herself. The game was over. She was not going to allow this any longer. She was a Cullingham. "No, my lord, for you see, I am *not* a jade."

"I want you to be my mistress. No one need ever know. We can be careful."

"*I* will know," she answered softly, reasonably.

"I won't hurt you, Arabella. . . . I want you."

"Do you, my lord?" She invited more.

"Yes, but I won't marry you, if that is what the silent question is." He shook his head. "I don't mean to be trapped."

"It is not my intention to trap you. I am not the sort of woman that takes what isn't hers."

"I could be yours in many ways . . . many pleasurable ways," he said on a seductive note.

"I am sure, and perhaps one day I will regret missing the experience," she said, and turned to move out of his path. She wasn't going to have her heart broken. She had to get out of his sphere. He was all too magnetic, all too desirable. After all, she was flesh and blood. Isn't that what men said when they wanted a women beyond reason?

"Arabella . . . ?" He frowned and attempted once more to stop her from leaving. "We were meant for each other."

"Were we? I am sure I have heard that said to me before, and no doubt you have said it to another," she answered sadly, and returned to the ballroom.

He did leave then, abruptly. He hadn't been able to before. Earlier he had reached the central hall and had somehow found himself turning back, going into the quiet of the library to think. Well, it hadn't served, and he was getting out of this blasted place. He was going to go to his club and drink himself under the table!

Arabella reentered the ballroom to discover Maria and James in a heated debate. It appeared that Felix had started it by informing James that he should not be dancing while Maria was in mourning. James was his own man and rarely allowed anyone to dictate to him; his answer had been sharp. Maria had taken umbrage and had petted Felix's arm at once, saying that Felix had more sensibility than James in this matter.

Arabella was diverted and eyed Rose with something close to pixie glee as Maria stalked off on Felix's arm. She moved to James and said gently, "Time to cry off, my dear."

"Damnation, Bell, don't I wish, but I am a man of honor. I can't cry off.

So saying, he moved off in search of something stronger

than champagne. Rose meandered to Arabella's side and said lightly, "Something amiss?"

"He says he can't cry off." Arabella's brows were together for she was in deep thought.

"For pity's sake. Of course he cannot. He may wish Maria at Jericho, but he is a gentleman and will not back out of their engagement under any circumstances."

"Perhaps she is less a lady than he is a gentleman," suggested Arabella.

"What is that supposed to mean?" Rose's brow was up.

"Never mind. Forget that for the time being and attend to me, Rosey, for I think I have ruined my life."

"He was so furious, Bell. I saw," answered Rose. "Shaun has a temper, and you certainly have ruffled it.

"He asked me still, knowing who I am, to be his mistress."

"He didn't!" cried Rose in some shock. "I can't believe it. That isn't like Shaun."

"I must bring out the best in him." Bell grimaced. "For that is precisely what he did."

Arabella was blue-deviled, but even so, there was enough to keep her occupied. Between dances she managed to find Lady Sefton and, after passing a few pleasantries, commented, "Who was that sweet-looking young woman you came with, my lady?"

Lady Sefton eyed Arabella inquiringly, for she was a London hostess and very little escaped her notice. "Ah, so you think it time to take a hand in your brother's affairs?"

Arabella's face fell ludicrously. "Never say his affairs are now common knowledge!"

"Well . . . one can't go about trying to stuff performing bears into coaches without some of the story leaking out, though I daresay it was grossly exaggerated."

"Did . . . did Miss Swindon tell you about it?" Arabella was frowning.

131

"Ah, so you *do* know her?" Lady Sefton's brow was up, but a smile was curving her lips.

"Well, I certainly know her name, but no, we have never been introduced."

"And you would like to be introduced?"

"Very much," answered Arabella openly.

"Then we shall accomplish that right now, for I have a feeling it is just what my dear Diana needs, though you, my love, are quite a reprehensible baggage!"

Oddly enough this hit home, and Arabella's smile vanished. She liked Lady Sefton, and her opinion mattered. Bell took her seriously and said at once with much concern, "Oh, am I, my lady? I have found myself so accused lately that I begin to think that indeed I am. . . ."

Lady Sefton put her arm about her at once. "Arabella, how is this? I don't think I have ever seen you so easily despondent. I was but teasing. You know that I adore you, and I have known you long enough to know that you know when that fine line should not be crossed." She looked at Bell then said, intently, "Don't you?"

"Sometimes," said Arabella sincerely. "The thing is that I find myself making up new rules as I go along . . . and I am not always in the right of it."

Lady Sefton laughed. "I don't suppose you could be always in the right of it. I have never seen anyone *always* in the right. I myself have now and then erred." She dimpled adorably and gave Arabella's shoulders a squeeze. "I have listened to your prattle since you were a babe, and I have watched your entrance into society with great interest, my dear. I rather think you have the knack for it."

Arabella felt bolstered. "Do you? At times I think so, too. Now, my dearest Lady Sefton, where is she?"

"Coming our way, which is just as it should be." Lady Sefton winked. "Better that she come to us." They waited for Diana to approach, and then it was an easy thing for Lady Sefton to make the introductions.

Lady Sefton started their conversation but soon found reason enough to leave them. However, she added as her parting shot, "Oh, Bell . . . do get Diana to tell you about the new grey Grenville purchased for her only this morning." Then to Diana: "You must know that Arabella is an avid horsewoman. I think she would love to have a look at him."

Diana blushed prettily; however, she was urged on by Bell, who silently thanked her ladyship for giving her a topic on which they would both be able to converse easily. "Dapple gray, is he?"

"No." She shook her head. "Snowy gray and a mare." Diana's gray eyes lit up. "With a sweet disposition, but I don't know that she will work out in the hunting field."

This time Arabella's eyes lit up. "Hunting field? Do you hunt?"

"Hmmm, whenever I can. When I started riding, my guardian took me along with him whenever hounds ran, and they tell me I started riding before I was even able to walk." Both girls laughed and fell into easy discourse.

This went on until Arabella's mind found the answer she was looking for: "What's that you say? You bought her without trying her paces through the fields? Diana . . . I know just what we will do!"

Diana was a reserved young woman. She did not bubble, and she did not use first names so readily. However, she found she rather liked this frothy girl and discovered herself warming to Bell's charm. "Do you? What shall we do?"

"Why, we will go on a riding party to Loon Meadows. It is a marvelous stretch of riding country just west of London. I have never been there, but I have heard so very much about it . . . and there is this quaint little coffee house we can stop by. . . . Oh, it will be such fun, and Cricket has been wanting a run."

Diana frowned. this was something she would have to think about. "I don't know. . . ."

"What do you mean, you don't know?"

Again, Diana found herself laughing. "Well, when do you think we should do this thing?"

Arabella gave this some thought. "Not tomorrow . . . We shall no doubt be rather dull after tonight's work, but the day after."

"I see . . . and who will be the members of this riding party of yours?"

"Trusting soul, ain't you?" teased Arabella. Then, because she could see that she had flustered the girl, she quickly put in, "No, no don't fret, girl. Rose—you haven't met her—she is on the floor with James. . . . See there." She indicated with her chin as Rose passed on James's arm. "Maria Yardley, Sir Felix Standish. . . ." She looked around for Felix, but there was too great a mesh of people. "You, I, and whomever you wish, of course . . ."

"A jovial number," commented Diana dryly.

"Too little, do you think?" Arabella was having such a good time. No sense mentioning that Robby and Freddy would be there.

Diana shook her head, but refrained from further comment as a pleasant-looking gentleman came to claim Arabella's hand for the next waltz.

Chapter Twenty-one

Arabella opened one eye and waited a moment before attempting to open the other. She had danced until the wee hours of the morning. She had had a trifle too much champagne and one too many of Violet's lobster tarts. Her one open dark eye discovered the pillow under her chin, and she moved onto her side with a groan. She was very sure she should close her eye again and so she did; however, the knocking at her door (the same sound that had roused her) was repeated.

"No," she said in general.

"Yes, but Bell . . . I want to talk to you," came her brother's anxious voice.

She had a great deal of love for her brother, so she considered his request, glanced at her mantle clock, noted that it was not yet eight o'clock, and answered him, "Go away."

"Bell . . . I'm coming in . . ." her brother warned.

"Try it with risk to your life," she threatened.

Not the least bit concerned for his life, he entered, marched over, and plopped himself on her bed. This did not get her to look at him, so he took action. He pushed at one limp shoulder and demanded, "Bell . . . I want to talk!"

"Robby . . . !" wailed Arabella, "Do you want to kill your only sister?"

For answer he got up from the bed, strode across to the drapes, and forcefully drew them aside allowing the sun's morning rays into the room in some abundance. Arabella groaned painfully, turned onto her stomach, and pulled the pillow over her head. "He does," she told the mattress in muffled accents. "He wants to kill me."

"I should kill you," he answered.

She thought this over and decided he was in the wrong of it. "Why, you wretched thing."

"Because, I saw you talking to *her!* What did you say to her? Have you done something outrageous?"

"Odious thing," she managed to put up her head to say, "I have done something wonderful, and if you don't leave me alone, I shan't tell you what it is." But by now she had thrown the pillow at his head and sat bolt upright in her bed with something of her usual vitality.

Another knock sounded at her door, and a kitchen serving girl appeared with a tray of hot chocolate and biscuits. Brother and sister waited for it to be set down on the nightstand and for the girl to leave before they started speaking again; however, their conversation was not in accord. Bell remarked upon the tastiness of the hot chocolate, and Robby said he couldn't. She would have it that the biscuits were buttery and delicious; he said watching her eat made him sick. She returned saucily that he could leave and not watch her at all. He answered that she was in danger of her life again.

This made her laugh and relent. "Well then, brother, if you have any plans for tomorrow, you must cancel them."

"Why?" He was frowning and looking very worried.

"Because we are scheduled to go on a riding expedition to Loon Park."

"We? What do you mean, we?" he asked suspiciously,

and discovered that his heart was beating at an extraordinary rate.

"Oh . . . let me think. . . ." Arabella was delighted and teased him on, "Rose, James, dear Felix, and of course my darling Maria, Freddy, and you."

He was frowning. "What has this to do with anything?" Now he was vexed.

"Oh, I forgot to mention that Diana makes up one of our set." She was biting into a biscuit and watching him with a sweet smile.

He stood up, sat down, and then stood up again. "She accepted?"

"She did."

"She wouldn't," he answered.

"But she did. I think she finds me . . . tolerable," answered Bell.

"Does she know I shall be there?"

"She knows that you are my brother and that you generally escort me about."

"Yes, but does she know that I will be there?"

"She has no reason to think you won't be there."

"Arabella!" He was now very close to shaking her. "She doesn't know . . . does she?"

"You are acting like a schoolboy. She will know soon enough when we fetch her tomorrow morning, and she is too much a lady to cry off or turn you up cold. Wait and see."

"Bell . . . you can't go about manipulating people like this," he said in some agitation.

"Oh, but I can, for just look what a mull people make of their lives. Here is this perfectly sweet and lovely girl mistrusting every male simply because one misled her. She should have the opportunity to reject you *after* she knows you. I am going to give her that opportunity. After that, my brother, you are on your own."

He studied her for a long moment and sighed. "I don't know. You make it all sound so simple and logical. . . ."

"Because it is."

"Whether it is or it isn't . . . I want to see her. . . . I need to see her, and I suppose I must be grateful. . . ."

"No, I wouldn't go that far, you dreadful boy, for if ever you become leg-shackled to her, no doubt you will find cause to lay that at my door, and I shall never hear the end of it."

He laughed at that, bent, and dropped a kiss upon her well-shaped head. "Right, then. I will inform Freddy of this . . . and I don't know how that will fadge, let me tell you."

Arabella laughed and waved him off. There was more, so much more, on her mind. There were James and Rose. She could see that they were in love and that they were both being very brave about it. Drat braveness. What good would it do? None. Something had to be done. There was the earl, her rogue, her cavalier. Something would have to be done in that direction as well, for she meant to have him!

The earl awoke with a start and found his man-servant opening his rich brown velvet drapes to display an alarming amount of sunshine. His hands went to his head and he groaned. Think, he told himself. You must think. This was because he couldn't for the life of him remember where he was or where he had been.

Someone was talking. His servant. What did the blasted man want? No, he didn't want his coffee . . . wait, coffee . . . yes, he would have his coffee. He managed to grunt, open his eyes, and pull himself into an upright position. The room made a circle around him while he watched in horrified fascination. Unsteady hands took the coffee cup being held out to him, and he sipped. He was home. Here was his valet, urging him to drink up and feel more the thing. That was right. It was his home. He had made it home last night. Where had he been? The Beau . . . the Beau had followed him out of the ball . . . Arabella's ball. He had said something about Arabella. Beau Brummell was not in the petticoat line, said women were too fatiguing to worry about, but the rumor was that the beau was breaking his heart over Lady Hester, and so it was. He had mentioned something of the sort and they had gone off to the club to drink . . . and drink, and, good lord, how many bottles had they put away? Arabella, a Cullingham? It didn't seem possible. When he had taken her up in Dorchester he had thought her a cit's daughter under the protection of Sir Robert. He had never looked any further. There had been times when he had wondered how she had acquired such refinement of speech, for hers was the queen's English. She held herself in such a way that suggested self-assurance in society, and he had marveled, but never had he thought . . .

Damnation! What a fool he had made of himself! And how the devil had she allowed it to go this far? Why hadn't she stopped him? Why hadn't he realized she was a Cullingham? Why hadn't she told him? She had allowed—deuce take it—she had led him to believe she was Robby's mistress. Why? She had given him kiss for kiss. Hell and fire! Arabella . . .

He couldn't think straight last night. He had been in the devil's own temper. He couldn't think straight now, for his head was fuzzed with the remains of what he had imbibed, but he knew one thing. It wasn't over yet. She had offered him something of a challenge and, by damn, he was taking her up on it! What did she take him for? Some flat without a comeback? She had offered herself up for seduction, and that was just where he was taking her, virgin or no!

What had she told him once? Something about having had a sad romantic experience. What was in that? There was certainly something in that. Did she know she was playing with fire? Had she done it on purpose? Why? To teach him a lesson. Ah, yes. He had come to know her in some ways, and that, he decided, was certainly something she might set out to do. However, he had seen something in her eyes, something that betrayed her desire. She wanted him just as he wanted her—and by Certes, he was going to have her! He found that he was no less determined, even now, when he knew she was a Cullingham. What did that make him? Never mind. He couldn't think about that now. All he knew was that he had to have her . . . and soon!

Chapter Twenty-two

Violet had not left her bed until noon, and then only to float about the house announcing that her ball had been *the* social triumph of the season. To her staff she not only gave a special thanks but graciously delivered sealed envelopes with a generous gratuity for each member.

She then went in search of Rose and Arabella and found them relaxing in the library with James. She eyed them for one long moment before entering. There was something she could not pinpoint that made her look longer, something about Rose; something about James that made her grow thoughtful. Perhaps it was the easy manner in which James was touching Rose's hand. Perhaps it was the style of her smile as she looked up and laughed at something he said. From them she turned to look at Arabella, and both her brows went up, for Bell had such a look on her face! Well, well, what was all this? She shook off her curiosity. Better not to know!

"My darlings!" she said in lively affection as she descended upon them, first hugging Bell and then Rose. "You made me very proud."

"Oh, Vi . . ." laughed Arabella.

"It was a lovely ball, Vi," said Rose sweetly. "Everyone enjoyed himself immensely."

"I have never attended a ball I enjoyed more," added James, coming to her and giving her cheek a pinch.

The library door opened once more and Fritzy announced Miss Yardley in his driest tone. He had come with the Cullinghams from the Grange and had never thought very much of any of the Yardleys or their household staff. He did, however, like James Huxley, who had been a frequent visitor at the Grange. He then announced Miss Yardley's companion, Sir Felix. Now that, he thought, that was more like it—Sir Felix and Maria Yardley. Ah, well, such was life.

Maria followed her name. Felix was close behind. She was looking rather radiant in a walking suit of pale blue and a pretty chip bonnet set upon her tightly braided hair. James looked up from Rose and discovered that his smile actually faded. There was something about Maria's eyes that he had never really noticed before. They were cold, so very cold, in contrast to Rose's soft, warm, hazel eyes.

"James!" Maria exclaimed as she nodded to the assembled company and went to Violet to drop a kiss upon that lady's cheek. "We have such good news." She turned to Felix, who was now bending over Arabella's hand, and frowned, forgetting for the moment what she had been about to say. She waited for Felix to come up from Arabella's hand and smiled at him, getting his attention. "Felix and I have found you a lodgings."

James's face fell absurdly, but he quickly recovered; he did not like his affairs managed by any other than himself. He had not asked Maria to look for lodgings for him, and he would not be manipulated. His brow went up in haughty style, and he said severely, "Really?"

"Why, yes. Felix knew of a small flat . . . a lovely place really . . . just near Kensington . . . and took me there this morning to have a look at it. . . ." She could see that James was vexed.

"Did he really? How very nice of him, though why he

should take you there is beyond me," James returned in frosty accents.

"Thought Maria might know whether or not you would like it. Didn't want to bother you about it . . . not sure it would be up to your taste . . . locale not quite the thing. . . ."

"Oh, there is nothing wrong with the locale," said Maria, "and it will do just fine for the remainder of the season. After all, we shan't need it once we are married."

"I find, Maria," said James in frigid terms, "that I don't need it now!"

"Oh, but James . . . you can not impose on the Cullinghams forever," scoffed Maria.

"Oh, but he is not imposing," said Arabella quietly. "He is and always has been one of our family."

"Oh, that is very sweet of you Arabella . . ." said Maria, nearly grinding her teeth, "but I know that you are merely being polite. At the outset, this was only to be a temporary situation. . . ."

"I think James must stay," put in Violet regally. "You see, we flighty Cullinghams look to his steady influence. I don't know where any of us would be without James to bear us company."

James smiled at her and came off his high ropes. "Thank you," he said softly, and then more reasonably, "but perhaps, Maria is right. . . ."

"Nonsense," said Arabella. "If you can put up with us here, we would prefer you to stay on for as long as you like."

"Then it is settled," said Violet, closing the subject.

Maria was angry, very angry. She seethed but she said nothing to this. Sir Felix fidgeted, for he had not liked the scheme of going to see the lodgings with Maria. However, he had made the mistake of mentioning the place to her last night and somehow she drew him into the outing. He looked at her now. It was really too bad she was engaged to marry Huxley, for he rather liked her quiet, regal style. Arabella bounced so much that she had his head forever in a spin. He felt much more restful with Maria at his side. . . .

"Good. Now that we have that problem settled, we can move on to the next matter. I am so glad you are both here, Maria, Felix. . . ."

The library door opened once more and the earl of Magdalen was announced. Arabella turned several shades of red before she went white. She sat rigid and watched him as he entered the room and moved to take Violet's hand. He was so very handsome in his light blue cutaway. His shoulders were so perfect, his waist so narrow, his body so tall, his legs in the buff-colored britches so athletic, and his eyes, oh faith, so blue!

He did the rounds, leaving her for last, and when he took her trembling fingers to his lips, it was to kiss their tips and wink. "Did you think I would not come?" he whispered.

"Yes . . . no . . . I . . . you left so early, and I thought you understood . . ." she answered in a hush, pleased that everyone else was talking and not involved in their conversation.

"Ah, love . . . you mistake me."

She dimpled. "You don't understand?"

He laughed and sat beside her on the sofa. She was looking a beauty in her gown of white muslin with her amber curls in a fluff all around her head. He flicked her nose. "We are playing semantics."

"Now . . . get back to what you were saying, please," Maria interrupted them.

"What is that?" Arabella had really forgotten.

"You said there was another matter to be settled," urged Sir Felix.

"Oh, that. Well, it is about tomorrow's riding expedition." Arabella answered, and then blushed, for she could

144

feel the earl's deep blue eyes on her. "I thought we should set up a time."

"Must we go?" moaned Maria.

"You needn't go if you won't like it," said Arabella with a smile.

"But James goes," returned Maria.

"So he does," answered Arabella.

Rose nearly choked and got up from her lady's chair to walk across the room and sit beside Violet, who was now ready to leave the young people to themselves. She patted Vi's hand and said softly, "You don't want to leave now and miss the fun."

"Oh, yes I do," answered Vi firmly.

"No, no," laughed Rose, "you must see your niece in action."

"Must I?" Vi moaned.

"Well, if James is to be one of your set, so then must I," answered Maria. "Besides, Felix says he thinks it might be some fun, and I rely on his good opinion."

"Ah, but not on James's good opinion?" returned Arabella still sweetly.

The earl was seeing another side to his Arabella and was greatly amused. Maria became slightly flustered. "That is not what I said."

"Never mind. We still need to set a time," answered Arabella.

James's eyes were twinkling, and he answered, "I think we should get started by nine o'clock. What say you, Felix? Since my intended bride, I am certain, would like to hear *your* opinion." He was getting in on the spirit of things.

Sir Felix saw nothing amiss in being asked his opinion, and declared the time of nine to be an excellent hour, as they would have to go and collect Miss Swindon as well. The earl watched this exchange with lively interest and interjected—for Arabella's ears only, as the others were now arguing over the earliness of the expedition's time, "Where do you go tomorrow?"

"Loon Park . . . and then Loon Tavern for luncheon," she answered without meeting his eyes.

He forced her to look at him by taking up her chin for a brief moment. "As I am here, would it not be the polite thing to invite me to join this party of yours?"

"You . . . you want to join us?" She was surprised.

"I want to join you," he answered simply.

"Then you are welcome—but I warn you, my lord . . ."

"Do you?" he interrupted. "Then, so I you, my pretty." He got up then, for he didn't want to give away his hand in front of Violet, and she was looking their way with keen interest. He couldn't resist bending over Arabella's fingers and looking into her eyes. "I will leave you, then, until tomorrow and miss you, my love, until then."

He then softened this pronounced attention he was paying Arabella by giving nearly equal attention to Rose. Miss Knoyles raised a brow at him and smiled a knowing smile, but allowed him his game before he took his leave of the rest of the company. When he had gone, James could not help from saying, "Well, Bell . . . looks like you have made quite a conquest."

"Nonsense," answered Maria. "Don't go and raise her hopes, James. It is a well-known fact that the earl is a confirmed bachelor and something of a flirt."

"So he is," said Violet gently, "but at the same time, Bell, he does seem . . . interested in you, and I cannot recall ever having seen him quite so . . . intent upon a girl just out. He isn't one that plays fast and loose with green girls, however pretty."

"Perhaps not," said Arabella quietly, serious, "but Violet, he is playing . . . only that. I may be green, but I am no longer foolish about such things."

The doors opened once again, and both Freddy and Robby came strolling into the room. "Wasn't that the earl we just saw walk off?'' asked Robby with a raised brow. He could still recall seeing his sister in the earl's arms at the theater and then dancing the first waltz with him last night. He knew the earl's reputation with women and had no wish for his sister to be hurt again by another rakehell.

"Hmmm," answered Rose casually, for she could see that Robby was not pleased.

"Well, upon my soul!" ejaculated Freddy. "What was *he* doing here?"

"Have a notion he came to call on our little Arabella," replied James with a wide grin. For his efforts he had a sofa pillow flung at his head.

"It won't do," said Robby with a frown.

"That is precisely what I was saying before you arrived," put in Maria smugly.

"Were you saying that?" returned Robby, irked. "Then perhaps I have been a bit hasty; perhaps it might do very well."

Maria's mouth dropped. Sir Felix shook his head and said severely, "Flighty pair . . . brother and sister." This was said into Maria's ear, and she nodded in agreement.

Arabella was twinkling delightfully, for she didn't miss a thing. Had she planned this incident, she couldn't have arranged it in neater sequence. "Robby . . . you will never guess . . ."

"I am certain that I should never do so. Better tell me then," he answered, moving over to pinch her cheek.

"The earl makes up one of our party tomorrow. In fact, he invited himself."

"Well, and upon my soul!" said Freddy again as he stopped pouring his brandy abruptly, "If that don't beat all!"

Chapter Twenty-three

Loon Park was a lovely stretch of wooded paths and open fields. Early summer flowers were in bloom, and wild roses lined several of the stock fence petitions, providing a charming setting for the Cullingham expedition. However, not everything went as Arabella so carefully planned.

Diana Swindon did not act with graceful composure and elegant decorum upon finding Freddy and Robby in their group. Instead, she picked up her riding skirt, turned away from her snowy gray mare, and started off.

Arabella closed her eyes and then set her teeth for action. She urged her horse forward, nimbly jumped out of the sidesaddle, and picked up her own black riding skirt, calling,

"Diana . . . don't be absurd."

Diana turned and put up her chin. "I am nothing of the sort. What I am, Arabella, is highly principled, and I cannot in good conscience associate with two young men whose conduct I find questionable."

"Oh, don't behave like such a prig, for I am persuaded you are no such thing." Arabella's hands were on her hips.

The assembled company, including the earl (who looked magnificent in his riding apparel of rich dark brown, with his top hat set rakishly upon his dusky waves) watched, though they could not hear what was toward.

Diana's eyes opened wide. "Is that what you think? Then perhaps you don't know the entire story . . . or your judgment is clouded by the fact that one of the young men in question is your brother."

"My judgment is rarely clouded by anything, especially by facts," returned Bell, hands now on hips, her tone belied only by the sweetness of her smile. "What I know is that all of us are human and not one of us is perfect . . . or do you think that *you* are perfect?"

Diana became flustered and relented, "No, of course not . . . but . . ."

"Do you think forgiveness an art delegated only to the gods?" Arabella was on her podium and thoroughly enjoying herself.

"Now really. . . ." tried Diana, reduced to the defensive, "Bell . . . you must see that their behavior indicated a wayward want of conduct. . . ."

"They were young men on the town and in their cups! Diana, haven't you ever been told not to do something and then gone ahead and disobeyed? Haven't you ever taken a ditch flying, without thought to the consequences? Followed the hounds till the end of the day . . . risking your steed's legs? Tell me. Does that show a propensity toward selfish cruelty to your animals?"

Arabella had hit home. Diana blushed, for she was an avid fox hunter. She attempted to reclaim herself: "Arabella . . ."

Arabella wasn't going to allow her to do anything but hang her head in shame. She didn't allow her another word but went on in fine style. "So, they found a performing bear and thought that I might enjoy having a look at it. I was at home and in my bed, so they thought they might give me a treat. They were foxed, Diana . . . befuddled with brandy. It happens. At any rate, the bear wouldn't cooperate, which, when you think about it, is a good thing, but never mind. They didn't get a coach to stop for them,

149

and the bear got testy and swiped poor Freddy. The owner had warned them about the bear's temper, and they did the only thing they could do—they swiped him back. That is what you saw.'' She was by now wagging an admonishing finger at her. ''Why you should not have listened to my brother's explanation is beyond me, for he is a dear, sweet, honorable gentleman.''

Diana looked at the toes of her riding boots and sighed. ''I have been presented with dear, sweet, honorable gentlemen, and they have all turned out to be otherwise.''

''So they have . . . but they were *always* otherwise and *you* were just too green to see it. This is an entirely different case. Now, we are keeping all our friends waiting, and that is unpardonable,'' said Arabella, managing the situation very well.

All this time, the earl of Magdalen watched the lady of his desires with some interest. That she had just handled a frosty young woman was a thing that encouraged his admiration of her address. That her facial expressions, her hand movements, the sway of her hips, stirred him beyond his imagination was something he knew would be fatal if not dealt with immediately. He went forward, dismounted, and aided first Miss Swindon to her side-saddle and then Arabella, his gloved hands lingering on her waist.

''You look delicious, little one,'' he said into her ear.

''And you, my lord, look better than any man of my acquaintance,'' she returned, a smile curving her lips and a twinkle lighting her dark eyes as she looked over her shoulder and then up at his face. She shook her head. ''I suppose it is the blue of your eyes. . . .''

He nearly growled, ''Arabella . . . ?''

She laughed and said, ''Come then, one, two, three . . .''

Some moments later they were proceeding in a sedate fashion out of the city's hubbub of traffic. It took a good forty minutes of walking and trotting their horses before they had Loon Park in sight and stopped to have a look at its entrance flanked on either side with wide brick pillars.

Arabella pointed to the first field of wildflowers and squeaked with delight, "Oh . . . look! Isn't it beautiful?"

In the distance could be seen a lake with a flock of swans gliding through the lily pads. The group started forward and the earl once again nudged his way toward Arabella. This suited her plans exactly, so she made no move this time (as she had during the course of her ride) to avoid him. She watched James and Rose converse animately before she looked up and gave the earl all her attention.

"Hallo, Blue Eyes . . ." she teased.

She was fast winning more than his physical desires, he told himself. This was going to have to stop. He would have to walk away or find himself chained to her heart. He reached out and flicked her nose. "What are you up to, minx? I have seen you work on this ride to some purpose; I just don't know what it is yet."

"Well, I hope no one else has noticed . . ." she said, biting her lip.

He laughed. "The thing is that they haven't. Are you playing matchmaker?"

She nearly choked. "No. How can I? James is engaged to marry that one . . . and Diana is sworn never to trust another man . . . and Felix . . . faith, Felix thinks he wants me!"

"And you? What do you want?" he asked gravely, though his eyes twinkled.

"A secret then." He nodded, and she dimpled at him and proceeded, "I want Maria to cry off and allow James his freedom so he can marry Rose . . . for it is plain as pikestaff that he is head over heels in love with her. I want Diana to forgive her guardian, and the wretch who hurt her, forget them, and then take a good look at my brother, who seems to want her. . . ."

"And Felix?"

"I want him to propose to Maria, for *they* are suited!"

He nearly went off into whoops, then controlled himself and inquired, "That leaves your life unsettled. Who shall you have?"

"Oh . . . I shall leave myself to the fates," she answered simply.

"And you are not bitter about that rogue . . . the one you once mentioned to me?"

"No. I didn't have my heart broken . . . just jarred enough to grow, and he was only an individual . . . not a representative of all mankind."

"Ah, Bell . . . you sorely try my control. You are a temptation," he said with a sigh.

"Am I? It is how I think of you . . . at night . . . when I am trying to sleep . . . I think how nice it would be to find myself in your arms . . . and not have to marry you . . . or anyone."

"Arabella!" he said, shocked. This was precisely what he wanted, to have her in his arms as his mistress.

"Well, it is what men do, after all. Take a mistress . . . and then, when their time is over, move on to the next one that catches their eye."

"That is different."

"It is how you want me . . ." she said softly, leading him to this point, "and it is how I want you, for I don't think I would be comfortable being married to you."

His jaw dropped, for he was dumbfounded. What new trick was this? However, she left him no time to think it over. She pointed with a laugh to a wide fallen tree, just under three feet in height, and said, "Look there . . . let us take it . . . abreast!" with which she began trotting her horse.

He had no choice but to pace his horse in time to hers and urge him on. They took their obstacle in fine style, laughing and calling to the others to do the same. Arabella was well pleased with her morning's efforts thus far!

* * *

The latter part of the day did not proceed precisely as Arabella had planned. A shame, but then things will go awry when one least expects it. Arabella was preening herself in silent self-admiration of her morning's work. How well Rose and James got along. How nicely Robby was behaving toward Diana, with just enough gentleness to win a smile. How well Freddy was behaving . . . just as he should. And the earl . . . well he was next to perfect. She watched Maria and Felix stiffly riding abreast and lagging at the rear and shrugged. Here now was the kink. She couldn't see that either one of them felt any amorous inclination toward the other. They were amiable and politely respectful of each other, but Felix still seemed bent on paying court only to her, not Maria. This was unfortunate, and due perhaps to the fact that Maria was engaged to James. Well, something would have to be done!

Just as she was working this notion about in her mind, the unexpected took place. Maria's horse was stung by a bee. The quietest, laziest of horses turned into a flaming high-stepper and took off across the field with Maria screaming hysterically. Arabella's eyes opened wide, and she watched as Robby, Freddy, and James took chase. She turned to Felix and said, "Do something!"

"Indeed, I think I shall . . ." said Felix. Moved to some excitement, he actually cropped his horse forward and into a gallop.

Ah, she thought, now if only Felix could be the one to save her, but the matter was out of her hands. Maria's horse continued to run, for now not only had it been stung but the poor thing felt chased as well, with all those horses on his heels and people screaming. It was onward for Maria.

The earl watched in grave thought until Maria's horse shied sharply to the left to avoid Sir Robby as he barreled

153

down upon him from the right. It was then that the earl made his decision and swung his horse wide to cut off Maria's frightened horse face to face. He stopped his animal and spoke authoratatively, but calmly. Maria's horse came to an abrupt halt, which nearly unseated her, and both rider and animal breathed hard as they watched the earl take charge. There was no arguing with this man—the horse sensed it and snorted as the earl slowly moved his own animal forward and carefully took hold of the reins.

Maria gasped and with her riding hat askew exclaimed, "My lord, that was wonderful of you . . . oh, so wonderful. . . . I was nearly killed. . . . I would have been killed if you hadn't stopped Brownie. He has never done that to me before. . . ."

The others had arrived and everyone began talking at once. Arabella watched Maria watching the earl, and her heart sank. Oh, no, this was not what she wanted, for she could see that Maria had formed a sudden admiration for the earl!

Later, during luncheon at the tavern, this situation became even more pronounced. Arabella watched wide-eyed as Maria openly ogled the earl and fell on every word. In some disgust she pulled a face and looked at Rose for a reaction. Rose controlled an urge to giggle and whispered, "Now what, my little planner? This wasn't what you bargained for."

"Oh, shut up," Arabella whispered back.

Felix frowned at Maria's behavior and moved his chair closer to hers, saying, "Maria, did you notice the lovely water fountain outside the inn. I daresay it dates back to the 1600s. What say you?"

"Water fountain?" Maria puzzled over the problem. "Oh, yes."

Felix was not pleased. Until this moment he rather thought that he and Maria shared common interests, and it nettled him to discover that she could be enchanted with a rogue such as the earl.

Then, as if all this were not provoking enough to irritate Arabella, Robby managed inadvertently to aggravate Diana. He was in the act of entertaining her with anecdotes from his school days when Freddy remembered a certain incident involving a peddler's monkey and recited the story for Diana's edification. She did not appreciate it and returned by saying that she found both Freddy and Robby had an inclination toward cruelty to animals.

"No such thing!" retorted Freddy indignantly. "We love the little beasts. . . ." He turned to Robby, "Ain't that right, Rob?"

"Indeed, Diana . . ." reproached Robby gently, "I think you take these things a bit too seriously."

"One must take seriously the care of creatures dependent on him." She went rigid with haughtiness.

"Oh, for pity's sake!" exclaimed Bell. "This grows out of hand, Diana. The monkey was fine—there was no harm done, and you do have an odd notion about these matters. Why . . . think about it."

"I think Diana is quite right," chimed in Maria.

The earl sat back in his chair and smiled, for he thought the entire conversation preposterous. Maria turned to him and inquired flirtatiously, "What do you think, my lord?"

"Why do you ask him?" demanded Felix. "One knows in advance what the earl thinks of such matters."

"Oh, take a damper," put in James with a laugh.

Felix was in a jealous temper, though he would have been hard put to understand why. He turned on James and expostulated, "And you should be paying closer attention to the actions of your future bride! If she were going to be my wife, I wouldn't allow her to make sheep's eyes at such as he!"

All eyes opened on that one, for never had they seen Felix moved to such heated emotion. That he was in a dither was obvious. Why, no one understood, except now for Arabella, who narrowed her eyes and took the situation under study.

He was jealous, she thought, jealous over Maria's sudden interest in the earl. Well, well, this was interesting. How, now, to put it to use? The earl had been watching Arabella with genuine amusement and leaned closer to her, for he sat at her left side, and he whispered, "What have you bumping around in that busy brain of yours?"

"Ah, many things," she answered evasively.

"I should like to go home," said Maria, pouting for she could see that the earl's attention was for Arabella and no other.

"The best notion you have had all day," returned Arabella, for Diana was sitting in quiet frostiness, as were Freddy and Robby. Rose and James had their shoulders together and their countenances, though lovely in repose, were quite sad with their shared dilemma. Yes, it was time to take this crew home and think of something to bring them all about! Really, she was going to have to think of something to save these people from themselves!

Chapter Twenty-four

It came to her in a sudden flash. Arabella was sitting with a cup of hot tea before her. The library fire was ablaze, for the day had turned suddenly chilly. It was nearly five o'clock, and she knew all at once what she had to do and how she was going to do it. It would take some finesse. It would take some dangerous dealing. It would take the earl!

Rose turned from her contemplation of the fire to look at Arabella and got a sudden chill. "What is it? Bell . . . you have the strangest look about you . . . ?

"Do I?" said Arabella. "I can't imagine why." She got up from the sofa and moved to the ornate black and gold Regency writing desk, where she sat and dipped quill into ink.

"What are you doing?" demanded Rose warily.

"Never you mind. Some matters are better left to me," returned Arabella.

"Who are you writing to?" Rose would not easily be put off.

"To the earl."

"What? Why?" Well, at least it had nothing to do with her and James.

"Hush. I want to get this done before the boys return from their club," was all the answer Bell would give.

The letter read:

Dearest . . . what shall I call you? I have called you "my lord" for so long, it seems the only appropriate way to address you. Perhaps, for now, I shall leave it as "dearest."

I have a boon to beg (doesn't that sound quaint?). You see, Rose and James, as any fool can see, are in love. However, as you know, James is betrothed to Maria, whom he doesn't love. Maria doesn't love him either, and in fact, at the moment, I rather think she is infatuated with you. In addition to this, I think Sir Felix has formed a tendress for Maria. A problem, yes? Yes. I mean to set things to rights and need your help.

I intend to have you all for dinner tomorrow night. I would like you to take Maria off to one of the private parlors and get her into your arms (you are adept at such things), and keep her there until I maneuver James into walking through the door. Voilá, the end of that engagement.

I shall await your decision.

Arabella

She sealed this missive and hurried to take it to a linkboy with express instructions to wait for a reply. She was sure the earl would be at home, for he had said during their ride that he was promised to his man of business for the remainder of the afternoon.

She was correct. He was at home, and he took her letter to a private corner of the room, excusing himself from his agent to read it. He read it through once, went into a whoop of laughter, called her a madcap outloud, and excused himself further: "I am sorry. . . . Give me just a moment to answer this . . . and we will get back to our papers." He then sat down to jot off hurriedly:

158

*Dearest devil (for I find that you are that above all
other things),*

*Yes, I shall do your bidding. But be forewarned: I
shall expect your gratitude in return. That is our bar-
gain, and yes, you may call me "dearest," but I
should also like to hear you call me by my given
name, Shaun.*

Your obedient servant,
Shaun

Arabella received this missive with trembling fingers and
read it through. Like the earl, she also threw back her head
and laughed. Devil, indeed! Gratitude, eh? Well, that left
a wide-open door. Gratitude could be given in many forms,
and so she would advise him . . . at the right time! Shaun,
she said to herself, and then out loud, "Dearest Shaun."

Hence, a new game began. She sighed over it and then
thought of Diana and her brother. This was something only
Robby could handle. She would jot off the invitation to
Diana, and then it would be up to Robby to set things in
motion . . . if Diana saw fit to join their dinner party.
Again Rose eyed Arabella and inquired, "Bell . . . what
have you done?"

"Nothing. . . . Oh, we are having an informal dinner
party tomorrow night. . . . Did I not tell you?"

"No . . . and I don't think you told Vi . . . or the staff
either," said Rose dryly.

"Ah . . . you are always so organized. Of course, I shall
go and attend to it immediately."

"Yes, but Bell?" Rose called after her; however, Arabella was already out of the room!

Felix was pouting. He meant everyone to know that he
was pouting. He had accepted the invitation to Arabella's
little dinner party, but he was not going to contribute to
conversation of any kind until . . . until what? He wasn't

quite sure. He knew he was unhappy. He knew that he resented James Huxley and that he was greatly disappointed in Maria's behavior toward the earl. Of all women, he did not expect *her* to succumb to the earl's charms. Of Arabella, he no longer thought. He had decided to let her down easy. She was a lovely, sweet, merry child, but not fit to be his wife. He came to understand this shortly after he had discovered Maria Yardley.

James was in a despondent mood. He knew beyond a shadow of a doubt that he would love Rose to his dying day and that being tied to Maria would be akin to life in hell. What could he do? He was honor-bound to marry Maria. He watched her chatting in a lively fashion with the earl and sighed. How could he have allowed his father to draw him into this tangle?

Robby sat beside Diana on the yellow sofa in the Cullingham library. He saw no one else. They were talking comfortably now in a light, easy fashion, and Diana's eyes were sparkling. He had no fault to find with his sister's little gathering. Here was Diana, ready to forgive and forget, ready to get to know him. What more could he want?

Freddy was sipping his light wine and gossiping with Violet. They were both enjoying themselves immensely, for they each had their own version of a recent *on-dit* to relate. Violet glanced around the library as they waited for dinner to be announced and decided her niece had put together a very lovely dinner party.

The earl gave one ear politely to Maria and managed to catch Arabella's dark roving eyes. His glass was raised to her in a silent toast, and she giggled. Damn, but she was looking beautiful in the simple gown of deep rich amber silk. She wore topaz in her ears and at her throat. She glided when she moved about the room, she bounced, she laughed, and she held his attention completely.

Arabella looked from him to Rose, who was talking quietly with James, and she sighed. Tonight she had quite an undertaking, but it was for her Rose. Violet would be upset, no doubt . . . but it would be all right in the end. Rose looked up and found Arabella's eyes. They smiled at each other. Oh, dear, thought Bell, if Rose knew what I was about . . . oh, dear!

Chapter Twenty-five

Dinner had gone smoothly. Conversation had flowed due to the excellent offices of Violet and the earl, who both managed to keep up a steady stream of entertaining anecdotes. The gentlemen retired to the library and were soon joined by the ladies. Bell was itching to institute her plan. However, the details had not yet been discussed with the earl.

She made her way to him when Felix managed to capture Maria's attention for a moment and said in a whisper, "I have an idea."

"What is that, my love?" His blue eyes sparkled.

"Don't call me that." She was frowning now, momentarily diverted.

"Why not? You are," he said softly.

"Love enough to take to bed? Yes, I know," she answered with a sigh. "Never mind that now—we have another matter to settle."

"Ah, yes, I am to seduce Maria."

"Certainly not!" she snapped.

"What, then?"

"You are to take her to the solarium. I will mention it, and you will be kind enough to jump at the chance to be alone with her."

"Of course," he said meekly.

"Then I will come along with James . . . but I shall knock, at which time you will somehow get her into your arms!"

"What then, my love?" He looked a charmer with his smile wide across his handsome face.

"Well . . . James will be able to break off the engagement. . . ."

"Will he?"

"He will have cause . . ."

"Ah, and the lady we have duped? What of her?"

"Oh . . . I rather think she was meant for Felix."

"Perhaps he won't want her if he thinks I have had her first favor."

Arabella was taken aback. "Oh . . . let me think." Then her eyes lit up. "No. Once James is home free . . . I shall tell Felix you forced the kiss upon her."

"And he will believe you?" He was clearly amused.

"Of course. He thinks you a devil, you see."

"And you?"

"And me, what?"

"Won't you care?" he teased, but there was a certain measure of gravity now in his question.

"About what?" She was puzzled.

"About me . . . taking another woman into my arms . . . giving her kisses meant only for you?"

She looked into his blue eyes and said softly, "I think the kiss you give to her will be nothing like the kisses you may one day give to me. . . . Does that answer your question?"

"Oh, my love . . ." he sighed huskily.

"No . . . I am not . . ." she said sadly. "You use the word too easily, without feeling. . . ."

"No, you are out there. I use the word for you. . . ."
There it was. He was in love with her. Here was this slip of a woman-child, and he loved her beyond reason.

She was blushing. "You tease me with such talk, and that is not playing fairly."

"I am not playing any longer. . . . Are you?"

She looked into his blue eyes. "Not with you."

"But with poor Maria?"

"Oh, yes, and please, she is not 'poor Maria.' Remember, she is engaged to our James but has been flirting outrageously with you for two days now."

"Ah, you are right, there." He laughed and then added, "Besides, I like James and Rose, and I have a feeling this dreadful scheme of yours might work." He shook his head. "That *I* should be a party to such dealings, though . . ."

"You agreed" she put in worriedly.

"Yes, I agreed."

"Then let us begin."

"Do you know, Rose . . ." said Bell, moving toward her friend, "I have forgotten to cut back that pretty flowering shrub we received this morning. . . ."

Rose frowned. "Flowering shrub? What are you talking about?"

"You know . . . the one the earl was kind enough to send to us. . . ." She turned and smiled at the earl. "Would you like to see it? We placed it in the solarium."

"Indeed," returned the earl. "I should like to see it very much."

She dimpled. "Then come along. . . . We won't be missed for a few moments before we take out the playing cards. . . ." As she passed Maria, she stopped. "Do you join us, Maria?" It was safe enough, for Felix was engaged in conversation with Violet. Timing, Arabella thought thankfully, was everything. Maria agreed readily, and the three moved out of the library and into the long corridor. They had only taken a few steps when Arabella said, "Oh, dear . . . I must go fetch my clippers. . . ." She looked at

164

Maria. "Why don't you take the earl along? And I shall join you in a moment."

This was so easily accomplished that Arabella's elation knew no bounds. It was, of course, destined to be short-lived, for they say those best-laid plans of mice and men, you know, rarely go off just as they should. She returned to the library and got James's attention by pulling on his sleeve, "James . . . don't ask questions and waste any time . . . Just follow me quietly out of the library . . . please." It was a whisper, and though Rose, some feet away with Freddy, did not hear the words, she was immediately on the alert. Something was afoot!

James had been a friend for too long to find anything odd about Arabella's sudden request. She was a minx, forever up to something. He chuckled and merely did as he was bid. However, just at that moment, Felix had inquired after Maria, and Freddy, who had overheard the plan to inspect the solarium, offered this piece of information. Before Arabella could do anything to stop him, Felix slipped out of the library with every intention of finding Maria!

"Oh, no . . ." Bell wailed, and took Jimmy by the hand, nearly running in Felix's wake. If only he does not knock upon the lead-paned glass doors that open to the solarium, all may yet be saved!

"What is going on?" James objected as he was dragged down the hall and around the corner.

Arabella could have screamed, for Felix's round fist was already sounding against the frame of the door. "Oh, no!" she wailed again.

Within, the earl had managed to wield Maria into a romantic position, so that when he heard the knock, he bent his head, took her chin in hand, and started to place a soft kiss upon her lips. Maria trembled, wondered at herself, and then suddenly went cold. She didn't want the earl! She was engaged to be married, and besides . . .

she didn't want the earl. Too late, the kiss was on her lips, and the door was swinging wide to admit Felix. He stood in outraged, jealous fury and seethed, *"So!"*

"Felix!" cried Maria, thinking in that moment her life was over. Felix, her darling, beloved Felix, had seen her in a most compromising position. What would he think?

"Unhand her, cur!" commanded Felix, moved to bravery. He took a menacing step in the earl's direction.

The earl had, of course, already done so. He was greatly amused, for he could see Arabella and James at the doorway and knew that his darling's plans had not proceeded according to design. Bell was already revising her script. Right, so Felix was here. . . . Never mind; that action was the same.

She pushed James forward and said, "You see . . . Maria has played you false!"

"No, no!" said Felix. "It is he. . . ." He was pointing at the earl.

"Do you mean to say the earl has played me false?" said James sadly, shaking his head in mock dismay.

"No, no. He has played my poor Maria false," said Felix, taking her into his arms, for she had lapsed into tears.

"Ah, I see. I thought she was *my* Maria. Who, then, am I to call out?" returned James.

Arabella nearly choked. "No, no James . . . you don't have to call out anyone. . . . Maria is the one who has played fast and loose. She came here alone with the earl after making eyes at him for two days and leading poor Felix on. Why, she is a regular flirt."

"No . . ." cried Maria, turning angry eyes on Arabella, "I never led Felix on. . . ."

"Ah, but you have made eyes at the earl," said James softly, "That I was witness to myself."

She turned on James. "And why shouldn't I? Ours is a marriage of convenience . . . isn't it?"

"Indeed . . . but I don't think it very convenient to either of you," Arabella cut in, perhaps a bit too roughly.

Maria gasped, took the ring off her finger, and flung it at James. "I don't want you. . . . I never did. . . . I only accepted because our fathers insisted!" With that she burst into tears again, and, sobbing, she pulled on Felix's lapels. "I want to go home, Felix."

"Of course you do," he said gallantly, and turned to inform Arabella, "You will be kind enough to give Lady Vi our thanks for a lovely evening. Miss Yardley is unwell, and I am seeing her home."

"Yes, of course," said Arabella sweetly. She waited for the door to close and turned to find the earl and James looking at her. "What?" she demanded.

"If we don't have a scandal over this last work of yours, Bell . . ." said James, still chuckling.

"Oh, well, that is gratitude for you, beast! Go quickly and tell Rose you are a free man and ready to make a slave of her!"

"Yes, Master Bell!" He laughed, took up her shoulders, planted a hearty kiss upon her cheek, and left her alone with the earl.

She dimpled as the earl gazed intently at her, and said again, "What? You don't approve?"

"Oh, I approve, my love . . . all too much." With that he took her into his arms, and indeed, his kiss was entirely different from the one he had just performed.

It was a long while before he released her, and she sighed against his hard, lean chest, saying, "I suppose I am destined for your bed."

He threw back his head and laughed. "Indeed you are . . . as my mistress . . . and my wife!"

She looked up at him, and his blue eyes held her for a long moment before he was taking her into his arms again, but before she allowed him another kiss, she said in a low

167

seductive voice, "Ah, my lord, a well-met match . . . yes?"

"Yes!" he growled, and then kissed her long . . . oh so long.

Love...
Romance...
Passion...

CLAUDETTE WILLIAMS